"The Oracle's book is incredible - the
has found, and what she has brought t
- Ray Gale, pilot, San Francis

"The Oracle writes from a place of deep feeling beyond the concepts and dogmas of traditional religion or new age philosophies. Her book brought me a sense of inner peace and confirmation of my spiritual path. The truth within me recognized the truth within her words."

- Colleen Cayes, M.B.A., Harvard University,
high technology consultant, Silicon Valley, California

"This magnificent book has you walk into unity consciousness reality now - knowing it, feeling it, being it, and living it. The Oracle shares the divine expression of love with all of us."

- Barbara Ann Curl, Honua Lani, director, Kauai, Hawaii

"The Oracle offers the very essence of divine wisdom in *THE ORACLE SPEAKS: Breakthroughs For Humanity*. Phrased in beautiful poetical prose that delights the intellect, her teachings rekindle the flame of divine love in the heart center and reawaken inner knowing while reminding us to listen to our soul's message. 'Behold the truth within and hold it in your heart.'"

- Marika Freedman, writer/editor, Hanalei, Hawaii

"Like a safe and benevolent lightning, this profound book connects the divine and material planes with startling, uncompromising illumination - joining the transcendent insight of the mystic with the wisdom of harmony in daily life."

- Foster R. Gamble, president, Energy Dimensions,
Aikido, 3rd degree black belt, Woodside, California

"The reader will find in these pages the power of allowing the divine light to co-create reality. This may be the last book you read, as you will now lead your world rather than be lead by it."

- Sally Illingsworth, counselor and teacher, New Zealand

"This book comes at a time when many are urgently seeking a balanced way to not just see or contact the light but to become it. The Oracle guides the reader gently and lovingly through the process of opening to the softness of the Soul, back to that sacred place that too many, for far too long have been locked out of.
In this simple yet profound book, The Oracle offers wisdom that shines from her total reliance on the spirit that guides, nourishes and unfolds each and every soul. And, in its simplicity comes its greatest gift - that "remembering" that stirs when we connect to the wisdom within our own beings."

- Leo Drioli, publisher, *Golden Age Magazine - for Personal Transformation,* Australia

The Oracle Speaks

Breakthroughs for Humanity

ORACLE PRODUCTIONS LTD.

Auckland, New Zealand   Kaua'i, Hawai'i

*Many blessings of love and thanks
to my divine complement, family,
and dearest friends for choosing
to share their lives with me.*

"Wishing you the best with your book." - Gloria Steinem

THE ORACLE SPEAKS: Breakthroughs For Humanity.
 Published by Oracle Productions Ltd., P. O. Box 3300-393, Princeville, Kaua'i, HI 96722-3300, U.S.A. Printed with soy based ink and bound in United States of America. First Edition. First printed 1995.

Library of Congress Catalog Card Number: 95-74758

Oracle
The oracle speaks.
p. cm.
ISBN 0-9648443-0-3: U.S. $12.95
1. Self-help. 2. Personal Growth. 3. Spiritual
I. Oracle II. Title III. Oracle Productions Ltd. (Firm)
212
1995

Cover design: Melody Cassen, New York
Cover photographer: Rachael Hale, New Zealand
Make-up artist & hair stylist: Toni Carlstrom, New Zealand
Final editing: Christine Young, New Zealand

CONTENTS

INTRODUCTION

"What is knowledge?" asks the Oracle. "What are truths? What is love? What is wisdom? Who are you? How can enlightenment be achieved?"

Not simple questions or answers for the human species to understand. Questions and answers that many humans do not even ask themselves or strive to answer. So many minds and so many thoughts occupying their days and for what end?

The Oracle Speaks is based on the wisdom of The Oracle and her conscious awareness. She brings with her eternal universal insights that can assist you, so that you become a fully expressed individual living a fulfilled life. The Oracle teaches how to use basic tools that trade old limiting distinctions in your mind for empowering expansive jewels of wisdom and universal law that support your real identity. In the new state of knowing, you will actualize yourself and model serenity, joy, love, harmony, happiness, stability, centeredness, beauty, innocence, and sincerity.

CHAPTER ONE

DIVINITY

THE AWARENESS

In these unique times, one often asks oneself about destiny and the journey of the one soul. The desire for some is to serve the many. The search to behold the truth for one's own soul is a multifaceted activity that occupies many for multiple lifetimes. All answers are simple ones. It is not for one to always question and to search for the answers but to decide how to ascertain wisdom and truth. Through wisdom and truth the solutions for resolution and harmonious action are found.

Kindly listen within to the pure messages of your soul for your empowerment into divinity. It is the great inner light that has given and regiven us all the ability to learn and grow in universal knowledge and grandeur.

This sacred knowledge brings breakthroughs and awareness, for upon remembering one's original emergence, one's original intent is known. It is in the soul's journey from formless states into states of form that separation from self-knowing occurs and thus the forgetting of one's intentions and emergence knowledge. Universal love, which radiates its energy as golden light rays from a profound and bright vortex, embraces us with its love, joy, ecstasy, wisdom and truth. When one integrates and aligns with this energy of love, a new level of living and direction becomes applicable to all areas of life action and interaction. *The internal dynamics that are fueled from the knowing place of the soul are generated from divine principles and sacred knowledge.* This gives respect and honor to all organic and inorganic life. Thus, a reality of achieving cognizance is realized and thereby nurtures one's soul and all with whom one connects.

Though viewed as a simple accomplishment by

those who are in divine energy and its grace, for many the struggle and resistance continue. Faced with multiple choices in daily life, the individual often perceives life through limited decisions, vision and expression. Confined by these restraints of the being, there is a sense of feeling lost rather than being centered, a sense of feeling lonely and apart, a sense of self-provision rather than sharing from the whole. Repeating the pattern of separation and loneliness further abuses the heart. Experiences that shatter the heart repeat themselves until the cycle is so ingrained that the opening for change and release is distant and difficult to reach.

As the journey continues, soft yearnings to return to soul loving and oneness still beckon. A recalling of pure love and divine grace begins to be received as small glimpses of the possible. A renewed reliance upon self-responsibility to grow and relearn rises inside the heart again, and the desire to return to the true self becomes stronger and redirected to the remembrance of the universal love and oneness. Finally, the surrender to the final stages of enlightened living takes place, and the realization that it is a simple shift to return to our true self is obtained and integrated.

The returning of the knowledge of self-responsibility for divinity realization becomes the awareness of the many, as the path of giving and regiving takes place naturally. Fulfillment and destiny are one action which not only soothe and supply the soul with love but bestow the wisdom and love to the many. For this we have come and this is whence we came. The blessed ones ordained by love reunite and honor one another and recreate and co-create a loving community with leadership reflecting the sacred values and principles that constantly radiate their message regardless of humanity's thoughts or idealistic phases.

Let us now reach a common place from which to rejoice in our understanding and knowledge of love and its great energy to manifest joy and harmony. The balance always dances with our rhythm, and the magnetism of the love energy always attracts beyond polarity to guide us home to our divinity. What a blessing it is for the gift of the magnetic pull to be attracted to the light until there is only light. Your awareness matures into a state of being that lives, nurtures and exists only in light. The power of the universe's love energy and its light will be known by more and more. It is based in each soul's desire and your individual commitment to surrender to its embrace - oh, what bliss to be one with universal consciousness and universal law.

DIRECT EXPERIENCE

No matter what the world looks like or appears to be through one's eyes, it is the deep inner message of loving light that actually permeates each being and thing. Depending upon the state of evolution of the seer, the beings and things take different appearances and meanings and occur differently for everyone. The idea of separation of beings and things creates a stage of interpretation, judgement and definition in which many become lost. When the move from original emergence and oneness is not recalled in each instance of living, then only the separation and loss of light are experienced. As the soul reintegrates and remembers its place, the learned one passes through the eye of the needle and returns to the fulcrum place of remembrance and knowledge of universal love. This love is the unity consciousness of oneness with what has been called God, the holy spirit and your enlightened self. When the light and its profound energy is received into your heart, embraced, and integrated, you can feel its sweetness, its waves of loving energy, and a filling of unconditional warmth that expands your soul. Just seeing the light is not enough. *It is in the full merging with the energy behind the light that brings full mastery. This unity brings clarity and evolution to the self quickly, as the envelopment brings one fully into the advanced state of enlightenment which I call "universal consciousness"* (a.k.a. advanced samadhi, nirvana, cosmic consciousness, oneness, holy trinity, divinity, spirit, God, enlightenment).

There have been many practices, rituals, ceremonies and teachings that attempt to define a process to develop divinity, but most are incomplete, erroneous and unserving. The search for oneness and wisdom cannot be found through another but relies upon the responsibility and willingness of each one to develop the strength to return to the self. This book shares practical, effective and simple ways to purify oneself and reach enlightenment. Upon this return, all skills based on love and truth arise and begin to manifest in one's life.

It is a tremendous commitment to reclaim responsibility and to maintain this commitment through the soul's journey which may take many turns only to realign upon the direct path of being in the receiving and regiving of the love. Reinstituting the sacred values and principles that are eternal takes great responsibility, as each thought requires a touch of purity, a touch of love and a touch of simplicity. The mastery becomes easy as your consciousness redevelops itself and your language improves. The mastery becomes a way of life without second thought as original thought is used. The mastery leads to divinity - our destiny; a breakthrough for humanity!

Overall, humans think in words, sentences and concepts too often, and ramble throughout the day. Attention is given to the minutest details and the most distant fantasies, and yet both are projected from the same central thought system of occupying the mind with words and ideas that are trivial and perhaps even harmful. Breaking this habit calls for a new practice. This practice becomes a way of life. It requires discipline to change and return to thinking in wellness and awareness of universal love. Without words, an artist or musician can evoke feelings of love, fellowship and connectedness. Equally, an adept can with consciousness make use of language, enabling one to take to heart the power and wisdom of sound and meaning of words to create feelings of love, fellowship and connectedness. In the communion with cosmic consciousness as a learned discipline and a way of living and thinking based in divine love, this way of speaking will always be a manifestation of pure personal character. Quite the opposite is practiced by most humans, and their plight is unrewarding and misdirected. Each relies upon others functioning in the same manner; blindness and enmeshment of unholy standards and deeds ensue. Throughout eternity on Earth, as well as in the energy universe, there have been and still are vibrations of unclear and impure thoughts constantly being regenerated by the beings and energies who have forgotten their holiness and sacred honor to themselves and to one another. This division only supports re-division.

The attempt to re-establish wholeness and holiness takes tremendous skill and responsibility. It requires the ability to step aside from indulgence and to reach into the decisive aspects of initiating salvation and redemption. When it does happen, the release of the entrapment of the previous thought structure creates the first steps into transformation. Consider these initial steps of inquiry as the bridge to that which was once too far to reach. Upon reaching its beginning, the redirection has already taken place. Making the necessary time to listen and fulfill the desire of hearing one's inner self becomes a function of the mind's surrender as it is gripped by the heart's command to unveil the soul and reintegrate. New peaks of freedom and nurturing knowledge will increase with attention and devotion to self improvement.

Engaging in relationships where others are also participating in the purification process enhances one's journey. These friendships embody the collective soul of the group, and a power of community spirit is co-created to benefit the members and others of the world society.

In the past, large organizations were founded to educate and relay information. In this modern day the massive tools of technology have created numerous smaller groupings to provide accessible and flexible service to the community. Small pockets of spiritual members share their insights and gifts, and the reliance upon institutionally directed information is being replaced by profound knowings of the responsible individuals. Home computers for writing, faxes for transmitting, cassette duplicating equipment, videos, IVDS, Internet, cellular telephones, cable, etc. all make it easier for anyone to share their message and speak from the heart. Individuals are increasing their self-esteem to self-direct and receive their knowledge.

Spiritual learning, however, is still only achieved by the direct experience of the soul. The rays of universal light and love hold and bestow answers to all of your needs. Even though technology communication transmits information through its medium, *the ultimate truth comes from within your soul and remains in your remembrance for eternity.* This inner knowing has always been the next step for humanity. Even now, as people grow out of the religious institutions, they too are growing beyond the technology dispersion of information. In this realization is the return to self-knowledge directly from the loving light to one's soul. Reliance upon anything other than the light in one's development is not necessary. Using the light will always serve and is always available. This access builds self-reliance and accelerates personal progression.

This oracular is a simple one. Behold the truth within and hold it inside your heart. Follow the deep inner feelings that lead you each step of the way to more of yourself, and soften. *It is not for one to rediscover certain activities of faith but for one to discipline the mental thoughts to relax so that the soul's message can be heard more and more.* The soul speaks of the divine essences and powers and repeats itself until it is fully embraced.

The time to begin always has been. Even now the entry through the sheer energy of light comes and shines to thee. And, for the spiritually adept, the wondrous ecstasy shines and radiates ever so brilliantly to be received in ever increasing bestowals and inflows that fill and supply the soul reservoir. With each wave of universal love your aura becomes brighter, your wellness healthier and the teachings more integrated and acknowledged. Self-direction in your destiny releases you from the control of confining ideas into the magnificent awareness of the cosmic laws and the blessings of love, joy and truth. Peacefulness and tranquility embody themselves in the psyche, and life is a forever magical dance, benefiting from these great gifts. I, too, was once obligated in the search, and now I am free. I, too, have had moments of the unknown, only to turn around and be enveloped in the ecstasy of divinity. Take the freedom and pursue your greatest passages into self-knowledge. Prepare for the next still moment and its gift . . . . love.

The silent moment to establish the recollection of the purity of divine existence starts with a deep desire to request the blessing and honorable grace of sacred bestowal of loving light into one's soul. Your sincere calling will be heard, and through the collective love of the divine energy, the gift of pure and unconditional love rays are softly sent into your soul's center. Through deep relaxation and sincere yearning, the light brings forth the homecoming experience - for some in a subtle experience, and for some in a dramatic experience. The difference is based only on the conditioning of the internal light corridor from the crown through the heart that is the soul's center.

Inner requests for further inflows of more intensified infusions can be made until the fullness and wholeness prevails. Continuous fillings for maintenance are very practical, as throughout your daily life the giving of your light from within can deplete your reservoir. Divine communion restores your reservoir levels and comforts your heart. In return you are able to give through regiving of this same light to your family, friends and community. Once filled with your own inner light, you come to realize that the unlimited supply of the love of our universe greatly enhances growth and creates a connection in a global manner that begins to provide for your worldly needs. By grasping this exchange of energy, you will learn to hear and see the truth and wisdom carried to you in the form of this light. The universal love energy is your greatest teacher, accessible by all and meant for all. It is a simple exchange, yet the most powerful and everlasting.

It was never meant to be a mystery, a strain, or a lengthy and trying search to be in enlightened energy or to live in alignment with universal forces. Through language and limited culture, large masses of people find themselves in an endless search for self-identity. It is not necessary to perform any bodily practices or mental mantras to achieve enlightenment or, as it is being renamed today, ascension. The soul can perceive and receive the divine love waves of soft light into the self at any level of awareness if only invited with sincerity and a willingness to be one with the love. Rather than trying to achieve oneness, I recommend a letting go of that goal as the focus and developing relaxation instead. With your heart, ask in communion or meditation to receive the universal love inflow into your soul and you will be heard. Your need will be supplied. The embrace will come to you consciously.

Making the time for the universe to hear your desire and see your commitment creates the environment of stillness that is needed to be able to see and hear the light as you are graced with its blessing. Let go of all attempts and practices of achievement. Your earnest, honest and open-hearted appeal with your inner voice will create the still moment. *The magnetic draw of your divine request will attract the sacred love to yourself, and the inflow will be bestowed.*

So simple is this way of being embraced, nurtured, renewed and loved by the holy light that humanity has forgotten. Be warmed and bathed by it and strengthen within. *Establish your center in the divine energy as this is your true base throughout eternity.* Feel how you increase your security and develop your self-esteem and sacred knowledge from the wholeness provided from this profound place. It is not for you to wander forever but to find your home in divinity and to radiate the light to others. It is for you to be all that you intended to be. It is for you to fulfill yourself by expressing your true gifts. It is and always has been the time for you to empower yourself and give in the regiving, to bless the community with your leadership and love.

You are not alone. The path of growth is a process, and the journey does end. The ever so bright divine spirits and angels continue to shine their light. It is a great pleasure to receive and radiate the light and continue to assist the many in universal love consciousness awareness. The love is so fulfilling that to be able to increase the potency is very rewarding. This is our heritage, to be in the light and to increase our receiving of the light.

The desire for purification of the mind is a noble one. The process is stimulating and humbling to say the least. Yet, so many find themselves involved in repeated cycles of unfulfilled living. These cycles become inflexible due to limiting mental distinctions based upon improper interpretations made when experiencing past uncomfortable situations. By holding one's attention to false distinctions and functioning in language, a loss of feeling of the soul's truth occurs. In this loss the person moves through life motivated and driven by the distinctions rather than by the directed feelings and intentions based in love and sacred skills that the soul provides. By ignoring the wondrous revelations and powers of the soul, the being slowly encumbers the journey and builds layers upon layers of disempowering experiences, apathy, and surface-living through the motions of physical existence.

As the soul reservoir depletes further, depression, loneliness and sadness are felt. People find themselves on a roller coaster of ups and downs through life rather than tranquility and peaceful living where life is an adventure. Let us absorb larger inflows of light and free our self-expression to fulfill our life purposes. Let us not dwell in the chambers of darkness and limitation but yield to the beauty of the universal flow of love and joy. Give yourself permission to be who you really are, and remember your truth!

With each refilling and expansion of the heart center, the mind begins to further relax and surrender to the loving feelings and intentions of our soul. In this state, the soul functions in oneness and cooperation with the great oversoul . . . universal love consciousness. When one is living from this powerful place, one acts in harmony and balance with the universal energies. The universal energies continue to bestow their gift of insight while their revelations continue to nurture your ability to see and hear in a new way. This new way is called living with sanity. For the holy ones are sane. The holy ones share their light and are caretakers of all life. We can all live in this sacred manner of being. It is not something to resist. The resistance takes much more energy than the surrender. *By freeing oneself to live by the light, with the light and in the light, authentic freedoms are realized, and the dance begins.*

As we aspire to greater depths and potencies of

the love, do not forget about the others who are in search of the same. Be the teaching example and share the way to this love. In your renewed state of divinity the great joy of sharing and bridging others to the light is a fulfillment beyond explanation. Wondrous heights of love and ecstasy are felt in the heart as friends and family are bridged into the loving light. The new levels of communication and relationship between beings of integrated honor, sacred giving and love acknowledge everyone. This acknowledgement nurtures all souls and supports the advancing growth into the light even more. To this, many of us have devoted our life teachings. Our service of regiving the light contributes to all, whether in form or formless states of consciousness, as we are all one.

As the regiving grows you will receive increases of divine light moving your soul into deeper potencies of the love energy. Often in communion or meditation you can find yourself receiving the inflow of energy and its light for hours. Upon opening your eyes you are surprised that what felt like a short period of time was much longer. The refilling and renewing of one's soul is such a relaxing and pleasurable experience that you can drift into it more and more easily. This is why I say the process is not supposed to be a struggle and effort. The universe wants to caress us all and we just have to be silent and still to receive the blessing.

The universal love is an energy that is genderless and timeless. It is not male or female. It just is pure love. Time is unknown to the universal love. It is humanity that structures time for organizing and synchronizing. Yet, divine leaders find that they do not use time like others. The natural flow of each day is very aligned and selective. It is like an inner clock guiding us through each day with great insight and natural timing. Living this way is living without negative stress, and you begin to feel and see the dance between the many opportunities of your day. This inner flow also sets moments aside for the quiet time to receive the loving light waves for refilling the soul's reservoir. I am always quite delighted and amazed how easy and free it is to live in divinity. What a treasure to be graced and blessed in joy!

I welcome you to sit down and sense the stillness inside. I ask you to listen to your inner voice and invite the holy light to flow in a deeper manner. Bless your being. I share with you my loving vision that you become brighter and freer each day. *Make your commitment to pursue the valuable riches of the heart and develop their magnificent powers.* You have all that you really need to begin, to continue, and to end the great journey. Self-reliance and self-responsibility will bring you to your full knowledge of yourself. This is the great task for all to achieve, and in this rediscovery you are loved and loved and loved!

In the divine remembrance it is very valuable to recall your original emergence and original intentions. From this knowing place you can continue through reviewing your past existences in form and formless states. Each phase contains wisdom and learnings to be aware of for this existence. On the average, properly regressing ten to twenty incarnations and the spaces in between will direct you to tremendous knowledge of who you are. You will evolve into a powerful space of knowing who you have been, who you are now, and who you can be.

The next steps to take would be to create options of what you can do to contribute your gifts and be in fulfillment of your expressions. The result is living successfully with prosperity, as you can have all you need by being who you truly are. *The authenticity of oneself dominates all outcomes and reflections.* We are here to unveil ourselves and build our self-esteem through the inner knowing. The inner knowing and being that is authentic and harmonious. Your self-discovery is your greatest ally and asset. By using the direct approach of learning and empowering yourself with the universal love, you can process very quickly and accurately. In this way you will save years or even lifetimes in your development. Make the time to know yourself, and rejoice in the freedom of who you are.

The universal love inflow is very measurable and

noticeable. Although one can experience peace, some telepathy, and visualizations during communion or meditation, it is not yet necessarily an advanced stage of spirituality. Many are on the spiritual awakening path and do benefit from their quiet moments, and yet there is more to be received and to be blessed with. *The universal love meditation bestows the wondrous energy and presence of the holy light. When you are graced with it you can actually feel the love flowing into your soul. You can actually sense the soft waves of love energy flowing into your body. You can actually see the light flowing into your crown. You can additionally interact with it by asking for more potent rays of golden light to flow to you. In the receiving you are in the energy and not in the thoughts or words of human language. This is the universal love enlightenment meditation!* From time to time some have received bestowal energy but they do not know how to reinitiate its presence. *It is available by your sincere desire and invitation to be graced by it. That and that alone!*

Continue to grow in this beautiful giving from the

universe. Your regiving to the universe is your growth into the realms of the divine love and its light. This exchange is the greatest love that can be shared throughout eternity, as it is the breath of life that bonds the universe.

LIFE PURPOSE * LIFE LEARNINGS

We have all come with life purposes and life learnings to be actualized in our unique ways. They are distinct and based on an internal formula created with guidance before each incarnation and upon the return to the spirit state between incarnations of form. The matrix pattern is woven to set the stage for your plan of growth and achievement. Sometimes you accomplish your goals and sometimes you do not. It is all a random experience of major and minor choice points. You never really lose. You continue on through eternity facing them again until they are achieved, modified or released. The challenge is to go beyond self-imposed barriers that limit one's expression and onward into the awareness of being the light and dancing in your purpose.

By coming to know and acknowledge your life purpose and life learnings, you are empowered to reach them with forthrightness, rather than just by chance. I have seen many people in private intensive sessions. It seems to be a human pattern to suffuse and diminish one's worth and true work. Many lack the courage and tools to fully blossom and be who they meant themselves to be. There is a giving away of oneself in the adaptation to the survival mode of civilization living. There is a pervading hope that someday it will all come together or be given to them. This is a powerless stand and the dominant factor that blocks most.

It isn't tricky or complicated to get to know one's true path and expression. If you envelop yourself with love and emotional support you can gain the insights and direction you were meant to unveil. The growth is in the unveiling and also in the outward action of the unveiled one. The after is as valuable as the before. The appreciation of the blossomed being is born from the experience of the unveiled timid person. Due to the lack of authentic modeling and the exaggerated hollywoodization of those who may have been authentic models, the populations are left without the leadership mentoring that is so extremely helpful. When you are surrounded by greatness you are able to present your greatness as well. Do not settle for what's so. Build the inner energy to be sincere and honest with yourself to reveal your real goals and desires. These will then through your internal processing of unfoldment reveal the mysteries of your identity. Upon the realization of your pure identity and wishes you will then be in touch with your true self and integrate and awaken your soul. Your existence is your soul and will always be. It is the hindrance that the mind provides by domination that one must stop trusting.

The vital key to successful individuation is the sheer will and desire to be what you really are inside. To reach your core self is to dig deeply and to bypass all curves, turns and hurdles that may appear in your reality. As you enter the sacred inner chambers of your soul, held so graciously within the heart, you will begin to sense that you are headed strongly in the right direction as it continues to invite you and give you energy to inquire and see. *You find yourself literally yearning to hear and know the secrets of your soul. Not anyone else's agenda, idea, system or philosophy will satisfy you.* Your own knowledge of yourself held inside you will be set free, eventually. You are bonded to it as your life force key. It will not go away and it cannot be lost. You reach a point where you can not stand to hear anyone anymore. You must *hear yourself inside speak!* As Robin Williams once said, "Be here now or get there later." I found that to be a very profound statement. The great seers and sages hear themselves and the universe. You can too.

What is it that is inside of you, protected and sheltered, that you are suppressing and not saying? Perhaps releasing some of the past emotional experiences held within will then allow a clearing for yourself to begin to emit and radiate your special message, talent and love. Do you want to uncover your true identity? Are you ready to be fulfilled and satisfied in a lasting way? Can you handle the success of living in wholeness once again?

It has always been your choice to believe in or to

model a belief. I choose *the ownership of modeling the universe's laws and love.* Serenity and happiness come from inside of me and are in a constant state of oneness with the universal divine love. My existence is held in the joy of the sacred energy that we are all made of.

You are not going anywhere. You are rediscovering who you really are. There are layers and layers to be shed in order to hear your sacred soul. The soul that has always been and will always be, you. Listen to your soul today and let it lead the way. *The power is in your hearing and seeing what it has to say, for it is the voice of your oneness with the universe.* You will see that you are returning to the beginning of yourself and that all that has occurred along the way is drama and acting. You can choose to become familiar with the deeper pure self now and refamiliarize yourself with your purpose and dreams. In regression or hynotherapy the soul memory is accessed to recall the past. It does not lie or play tricks. It is very focused to guide you to the next important memory to help you to rediscover yourself. In the rediscovery you will break through limiting thoughts and erroneous distinctions. You will gain wisdom and knowledge which will further enhance the search of the self. As you grow clearer and purer it will be easier and easier to be your unveiled and empowered self. The mastery is the knowing. The mastery is the capability of bringing oneself from 'out there' identity to the 'in here' identity of the soul. You will know it is your soul speaking as it is the sage within. Your soul journey will come to that protected, secret, still place inside - the wellspring of loving light. This is the place where you will hear your pure soul speak to you of your life purpose and life learnings. You will hear what you need to do to further evolve and enhance your life. You will hear your deepest desire and needs that are great gifts to be shared with humanity. It is in this place that you will manifest your 'ageless identity' and see what you have come to share with the world. You are relaxed in this space and feel embraced by divinity to illuminate yourself. The soul's journey never ends and it has never gone anywhere. The soul is a constant in the universe. We are each a part of this magnificent holographic reality. Do not allow it to control you and deceive you. You are an eternal being of pure light that experiences the oneness through your soul self. Learn about your soul and integrate.

It is not hard work to evolve. It is a simple process of stopping and giving yourself permission to listen to your soul's speaking. Humanity takes great pride in all of the external communication devices it has invented and marketed. Yet, humanity is starving for love, affection, attention and knowledge. Would it be possible for you to turn off all of the electricity for a few days and reexperience yourself instead? The civilized world's perception of living is consumption, doing for the self and judging others. The spiritual perception is loving oneself, loving others and being kind to all species. There is nothing to gain through things; they can only supply ease and comfort. The gain is how you perceive yourself in the world and your relationships with people and things. When you know your purpose and have accomplished your life learnings your perception of the world is 180 degrees different than it was previous to your awakening. With the reintegration of your truth you become a new rewired person that feels solid and directed and will not be swayed by those who hold 'beliefs' and not the knowing. This is the place where you impact humanity without effort or attachment. You literally are riding the wave of the universe and your speaking and actions are of the universe. This is the lifestyle of the evolved human that is an opportunity for everyone to integrate and model. Everyone has the choice to begin their mastery and uncover their life purpose and life learnings.

Your life will change immediately when you reconnect with your soul truths. You will begin to live by your identification with the image of yourself held within the pure energy of your soul. You will stand for who you are and persevere with your message and gifts. This is your greatest stimulation and source of self satisfaction. You have known these sensations before and will recall them. The benefits of knowing and living from this knowledge as your base foundation are numerous and immeasureable. The solar plexus area of the body carries your inner gifts, talents and forms of expression into each incarnation. To lift the protective shield to reconnect with them is mastery. This is the grounded center of the body. When you feel safe, your system allows this knowledge to flow into the heart, further up into the throat; and into the third and fourth eye energy centers. Your heart will know what you want to do and your soul will use the brain to bring it into words and manifest form. As you learn to clear the inner energy corridor with universal light you will be removing blocks of grey energy fields of limiting erroneous distinctions you have brought in with you. With each removal your self knowledge is gained and the creation of your self-expression for life purpose fulfillment begins to materialize. With your soul realization, you will be fully aligned and moving with the flow of the universe. All will come to you easily and perfectly. In a world based on external sensation and information, many are mesmerized with material mastery. It is the internal unveiling that will bring your greatest accomplishments and fulfillment. You will carry these powers with you and demonstrate them throughout eternity. Does it make sense to familiarize yourself with your own internal perfected skills that you have carried into this life? Would it benefit you in drawing a fuller picture of yourself to know where you have been before this time and what you have been? If you could relax your mind and give your soul complete permission to unfold and exist in a conscious manner, you would hold all keys and answers for yourself. All the learning of who you are, your life purpose and life learnings will not be found outside of yourself. They can only be generated within you and heard with your inner ear and seen with your inner sight. The visions are there and you can access them quite easily once you learn to meditate or commune accurately with the universe. There is so much to be accessed and retrieved.

The inner journey is a self-reliant one. It is simply a process of stopping and relaxing to sincerely listen to your soul's soft inner speaking. Your soul communicates through words and loving waves through your chest and your brain. By letting go of the internal chatter and external preoccupation with things of the world, you will enter the kingdom of truthfulness inside yourself. Your greatest strides are made when you listen to your soulself. You too can complete the course. You have all the tools to do so. Many of you are mid-journey. Some of you can see the light at the end of the tunnel and know you are coming into completion. I honor all of you for all that you have worked for and provided yourselves so far. I further bless you to continue forward in your unlearning of the past and re-absorption of universal law, wisdom and truth. It is here that the greatest knowledge will be assimilated and uniquely re-presented to the world. Your home, your freedom, your wholeness, your answers are held in the soul's center located at your heart. You are the one to create and establish your eminence. As you gain the strength and drive to complete the journey you will be energized to speak of your path. Each is different and customized for the individual and all hold the same workable and valuable tools of will and desire for clarity and purity. Be not lost in the world, lose yourself in your soul. Join the wondrous ecstasy of non-separation with the universe and ride its waves of love and joyous harmony.

SPIRIT GUIDES * ANGELS

You are loved. You are loved by many who you do not see, as they are on the other side. They are sacred spirit guides, guardian angels, masters, teachers, friends and family who are in the formless energy state, guiding you as you sleep and as you are awake. Your bond is very strong and deep with these special ones. They advise you in active meditation and communion. You have communication actively going both ways. The way to meet and access your spirit guide(s) is to sit quietly and go into your peacefulness and ask them to join you. With your inner vision you can see their loving energy of light and sometimes the shape of a more materialized form. You telepathically exchange thoughts of inquiry and speak of concerns and desires. In return, they will give you a larger perspective, outlook or insight. The wisdom is profound. It will guide you into alignment and positive progression. You will save years of stress and tangent distraction. Your guides constantly bathe you in healing and loving light. They not only guide you, they guard you as well. You are in their care and they give their care voluntarily.

All is on a giving basis in the universe. The absolute sharing process takes care of everyone's needs and allows everyone to be fully expressed. The receiving is demonstrated in this cycle. All are directing their energies to each other with 100% affection and unconditional love. The outward movement is a forward movement and is forever flowing omniversally. It is a feeding and nurturing that surrounds everybody and everything. To consciously be a part of this grandeur is to be an adept in spirituality. Your spirit guides and angels respond to your every need whether you hear them consciously or not. They know that one day you fully will.

Your spirit guides and angels live for loving service. All of their activities are to direct you to the best outcome in a holy and universal way. They are fulfilled by your advancing evolution, for as you advance you begin to model what they model and can lead the way for other humans. There are spirit guides and angels in human embodiment also. They are evolved beings who choose to return over and over again to be of service. They come in many shapes, sizes and backgrounds. You know who they are by their kind modeling. They support healing and love. They are the peacemakers and the leaders for fairness. They demonstrate clarity and generousity. They live as celestial beings in a grounded manner. You are surrounded by spirit guides and angels. You can see them if you wish to look. Their combined skills and insights can give you tremendous boosts in your spiritual evolution. They are demonstrating their purposes to the fullest. Acknowledge their presence and receive their guidance. You will be enriched in the exchanges by feeling cared for and loved. Your self-esteem will grow in the relationship and you will further yourself inside and out.

Your spirit guides and angels can assist you clearing away thoughts that do not serve you. In your meditation you can commune with them and receive another perspective on your ideas, habits and preferences. They will address matters very specifically if you request it. The specific knowledge then teaches you and you discard limiting ideas for new empowering wisdom.

CHAPTER TWO

CLEARING THE WAY

THE GOAL?

There are times in almost everyone's life when they have felt a pure sensation of joy bursting from inside through the heart. This is felt as a sparkling and radiating feeling of energized love and euphoria. It is often spontaneous and fleeting. It is experienced in a moment of great freedom and celebration. The chemical secretions of loving nectar fill the body and it is glorious. Welcomed and remembered these experiences are. They have been written about extensively through the ages along with descriptions of greater and longer enlightenment epics by faithful beings who had been searching for such.

Yet, for the many, the greater enlightenment

experience is elusive. They search, yearn, desire, strain, prostrate, cry, demand, and push to have a powerful mystical enlightenment experience. Philosophy, religion, cult, and history all tell of these episodes of the few and their lifestyles and perhaps contributions to the world. Some are myths and some are true. I often hear the question, "What about me?" or "How can I experience enlightenment?." So much emphasis is put on achieving the bells and whistles of the mystical euphoria that large populations actually believe this is their life goal. Many believe they have had this same goal for many incarnations and that it is difficult to achieve.

The lesson is not in the search or in the often stimulating sensations that will occur from time to time. The lesson is not even in having the goal. The lesson is, *It is not all that it seems.* Do you understand? *Even though the contemporary pervading direction is the search and the goal, I say that these in themselves are veils in human thinking.* As Shakespeare said, "Much ado about nothing." Some of you are saying, how can I say this? From knowledge comes the truth. The truth is that your forebears and peers are repeating outdated cycles. It is not for one to search and feel pain in one's heart. It is too easy to follow this pattern. It was never meant for you to be a follower of former patterning or outdated religious structure. You were always meant to be a brilliant child, a prodigy of nature and the universe, growing into adulthood as a caretaker for all life and bonded with all energy and universal flow. You were meant to be carried by your heart in love through each choice, thought and action. Your life was designed to be simple, balanced, carefree and joyous.

"Why isn't it this way? What happened?" Through separation, the wisdom was lost. Over-population began and further separation developed. Peace exists easily in a context of a small human population where the mind can handle all events and hold wisdom rather than remember or learn with the technology of writing, reading, printing, photographing, computing, telecommunications, etc. The exponential pressure of today's 'modern' living is a juggling for survival. Those who are in enlightenment and peace usually live simply and without the productivity deadlines you can have in your daily cycle. So, all in all, my answer to your questions is, *"Rely upon yourself, serve yourself and enrich your life with a strong focus on meeting your security, satisfaction, and relaxation".* This detachment from the search and goal patterning will bring you greater leaps in transformation than you have been able to access through the old process. Leave it behind and release your self esteem. Permit yourself to unfold and be who you are in the world. Then, your contributions to yourself and others will be sharings that are authentic and empowered in the alignment of the universal flow.

COMMON ISSUES

Humanity has to develop beyond self imposed limitations and breakthrough to self-realization. The following are many of the common issues that are cleared as one advances along the path to enlightenment. Kindly reflect on them and grow in your self knowledge. These are only to help guide you and to give you direction in seeing what are perhaps your own deep inner issues.

The issue of accepting to be here.

We have come to the planet to learn, share, play and love. It is our choice to return and be sacred human beings in this magnificent universe. We are provided with the beauty of the land and her loving essences that nurture our bodies and souls. We are fortunate to be able to have such a grand system of balance to reflect our consciousness to us in every physical and emotional manner. It is this reflection that often gives certain ones the challenge to be here and the questioning of wanting to be here. Even though one may be on the spiritual path and quite developed, there can still be an unresolved issue of accepting to really be here in this physical plane. It is one of the biggest and most common resistances that people have, and some aren't even aware that they have this distinction. Once the discovery is made that the acceptance of this choice has been in resistance, due to fear or other reasons, the uncovering of the cause(s) for this distinction appeal to you to be processed.

Feeling safe and secure in this physical world can

be achieved through regression into your personal soul history while being guided by the loving light energy. That is why I say it is extremely powerful to know who you are, as your coming-from place inside may still be carrying limiting thoughts from the past. Without the full acceptance to be here, there is a loss of complete willingness for participation and realizing one's goals for life purpose achievement. The underlying causes for the fear can be very hidden within the language of the mind's past. Once the review and clearing has taken place, there is a renewed freedom with the empowering awareness, and the love can flow into the energy space where the former resistance holding existed. With this increasing of the light, your life will shift forward in many directions, and your celebration for this life can begin!

The issue of giving one's power away.

Another major issue to clear for unfoldment and blossoming of one's loving spirit is the occurrence of giving one's power away to certain exercises, systems, or teachers. The habit of devotion and worship can mask a neediness and can misdirect and block one's growth. As I have said before, transformation takes place within and can only be achieved as an individual establishment of knowing. It is fine to receive occasional guidance and to commune or meditate in groups, but it is a weakening of one's self-development to create a distinction in the mind that supports a divisional class of student and teacher. We are all students and children of the universal love growing in the light until full enlightenment is realized. To worship and adore another human, idol or saint sets you to a lower class level. The universal love has no class system. It emanates love into the universe in a constant state of ecstasy to all species and matter.

Many find themselves in devotion and worship for lifetimes. Instead of spending hours levitating and adoring beliefs or beings, learn to focus on your own inner light and being in the light instead. The holy light has never asked for devotion. The sacred love asks nothing of you. The universe, will however, bestow to you the eternal light upon your sincere invitation. The divine love knows we are one and that you are a part of the divine energy already. The separation and state of devotion to teachers, systems, or exercises is a mental device to make the devotee feel some sort of achievement and discipline in their spiritual practice, but it is not a direct experience of enlightenment. Enlightenment occurs on an individual basis as your soul bonds further *in a direct manner* with the loving light. It is so simple. It is not necessary to go through another to be in the light. The light is yours to have now and directly. Please hear your soul cry out to be in this grace and state of oneness. Learn to relax your mind in further direct receivings of the universal love inflow. The light will always feed your soul directly, and to affiliate oneself in this responsible exchange builds self-reliance.

When a devotee comes to a teacher, there is an

exchange of love, depending on the evolution of the teacher. There are many masters, and most are not known. A following does not designate the purity of a teacher. Better to get in touch with the direct route. It is so simple and so informative that the intensity progresses you quickly.

Know that you are the key and the center of your universe. Learn to draw the wisdom and revelations to your being through the universal love directly. Go beyond even the "channeled" messages of others and learn to *integrate and embody* the love and truth within yourself. Enhance your abilities by directly using the light to fill your heart center until your entire body is one large field. In this wholeness you will stand tall and radiate your light by just being who you are in a natural state and not be lost in stages of devotion.

The issue of attachment to making a difference.

This has been a very common issue among people providing services and products for change. To serve for the benefit of the whole is noble when it is given freely with love. It is ego driven when motivation is perpetuated with attachment to the type of work or outcome in the work. *Any form of attachment is a dependent action rather than a free regiving of positive service.* Do your work from being who you are and not with a concern for making a difference. Changes will be evolutionary as a by-product of who you are being naturally.

The issue of not allowing yourself to be who you are.

An additional issue that many have is the fear of unveiling their power and telling the truth of who they really are and what their gifts are. No matter how special or unusual, there is a tremendous resistance to exposing oneself in this world. The fear of harm and disapproval creates a strong suppression of self-identity. Repeated experiences of being harmed, sequestered or murdered in past incarnations perpetuates fear and suppression of the self in future existences. To be happy one must be free of all the veils and radiate one's energy and image. Please learn to love yourself, nurture yourself, and build the strength to unveil and participate fully with the others who are in the self-knowing. The acknowledgment and appreciation that is shared will transcend any of the past limitations that hold the suppressive lifestyle in place.

The issue of adding meaning and interpreting through meanings.

Another issue that is predominant in this world is attaching meaning to everything. People do this through thoughts and words and then seek to create agreement collectively to the human made meanings. Many are misled by these interpretations, and the language creates distinctions in the mind which inhibit the soul's expansion, feeling and expression. Meaning contributes to inhibiting integration of the self with the cosmic consciousness. Ideas are created that block the feelings of soul love desiring to be expressed. How can it be that red is a holy color in one culture and purple is the holy color in another? How can it be that the number 18 is a holy number in one religion and another religion does not use numbers? Is one who is born on October 3rd more holy than one who is born on July 11th? Is the shape of ones body more "advanced" than another body shape? Am I sitting in the "correct meditation position" and "breathing correctly" for the eventual ultimate experience? Are prayers superior to meditation? Is Lemuria advanced and easier to dream about than facing where you are today?

We have always been in a magnetic attraction to grow further into the magnificent light. The universe does not care what color clothing you are wearing. It does not care what number your name and birth date add up to. It does not care if you are reading or hiking at the moment. It doesn't care if you are round or triangular. It does not care whether you are sitting, standing or lying down to receive the inflow. *The universal love just is and that is what it is. The love is always there, and the degree of intensity from which one knows it increases as one further opens to receiving it and being an example of it.*

So, listen to your thoughts and take note of the many meanings that are attached throughout the day. Begin to "observe" your thoughts. You will discover much about your mind and yourself. Then, learn to listen to the energy and begin to feel the loving energy of the cosmic divine love that occurs and exists *before your thoughts, before your creativity and before your words. Be sincere to yourself! Rediscover your true thoughts from the soul's love.* As you recall them, you will be surprised how you can relieve your mind of misrepresentations, time consuming meanings, and misidentifications that only separate you from your spiritual living in the light! Your continual blessing of feeling the love inside your soul's heart is a constant in the universe. It is up to you to build your self-esteem and to manage your growth to this wondrous level of knowing and sensing of the exchange. *Being free of the meanings helps you to operate from the heart. What a joy!*

Do you see how simple it is when the meanings are reduced and erased? Is it not a wonderful experience to feel, express and see only love? Yes! I say that living in divinity is our destiny. The giving and regiving of love is our greatest pleasure to express. Oh, what beautiful thoughts of wisdom and the love it endears our hearts with. *Your thoughts become words from the soul's heart and feel like they are coming straight out your lips - as if bypassing the brain!*

The issue of non-soulmate relationships.

Still another common issue is the predominant partnering with another who is not one's divine complement mate. This issue is so common that people begin to think that this is the way it has to be and settle for someone who is not their wondrous reflection but what is referred to today as their codependent reflection. To create and establish behavior to attract your life partner and dearest friend with pure values and sacred principles is a tremendous learning. The integrity for living from this place of divine being can permeate all life choices. With patience and the willingness to grow, the opportunity to shed the past limiting behavior appears and you begin to find your way to your true mate. Accelerated learning is the key benefit from using the loving light for inner growth. The outcome is the actualization of sharing this life with your divine complement mate.

Know that as you draw from purer spheres of consciousness, you will attract a partner who is also in the like vibration. There are many beings who vibrate from the same level of consciousness as yours. Do not limit yourself by searching for "the one" soulmate or twin flame. There are many of the same advanced vibration that can fulfill you and embody your dreams. Take your time before you make your final selection of the one to merge with. You will know. . . . .

The issue of substance addiction, anorexia and bulemia.

There are common behaviors that suppress evolution. To habitually inhale, smoke, drink, or inject a foreign substance into one's body are actions to numb the senses. Likewise, to undernourish or overeat and expel are unnatural actions for human health. In this numbed state, one can avoid the hurt, sadness, fear, low self-trust, and low self-esteem that lie underneath these symptoms. The avoidance can be so severe as to incur early death. The wellness and overall functioning of the human system depend on wholesome living. To redirect unloving thoughts and actions toward oneself is an example of a person in great pain and separation.

The lifestyle of this form of habitual behavior controls the individual, and the individual is no longer in control of their life and body. Their understanding of life, self-expression and how to exchange love is confining and confused. The spark of light within the individual must be re-attracted to the sacred light to start a healing process. Self love must be ignited once again so that they take back their power and come back into control of their lives and treating themselves with genuine love. The knowledge of the cause(s) will be unveiled as the growth process brings balance and healing.

The issue of violence and harm.

When people lash out with might, they are saying that they would rather hide behind weapons and fists than speak from the heart and co-create peace. They short-circuit their native intelligence and engage in actions of survival by strength and elimination rather than living from vulnerability and empowerment. The modeling for these people has been violence and harm. They have been weak within themselves not to have discovered on their own the difference between right and wrongdoing. The biggest effect is upon themselves in that they live without the experience of love and kindness and in their naivete draw only fear, insecurity, anger, frustration and hateful emotions into their sacred cells.

To grow beyond this level takes considerable desire to improve. The mental conversations that have been running them in circles must be identified and understood as reactive or erroneous distinctions. Then the unveiling of the causes in the soul history can be reviewed to grow beyond the recycling behavior pattern.

They do not know unconditional love. What a challenge to grow from this state into the light, to let go of reactive behavior that is only defensive and move into serenity and peace by clearing the deep causal issue(s) within, trusting and using the universe's love energy as a teacher and partner to self-discovery and wellness.

The issue of the fear of death and dying.

One more major issue is the fear of transition. The shift from the physical body into spirit energy is an unknown happening and the circumstances are unknown for most of one's life. The fear most often is driven from past experiences of painful and hurtful body deaths caused by suicide, murder, war, starvation, disease, etc. Yet, the spiritual ones have available the inner ability to see the light realms, and once the conscious understanding of a beautiful and profound release into the welcoming arms of the light becomes accepted, the fear dissipates. To learn to accept transition as a positive occurrence can lead one to review past transitions and understand the *circle of life.* Those whom have had loving near death experiences also know this.

Through trust and love the tunnel magnetically draws your soul being into deep loving energy as you let go of the attachment to the physical body. Those whom you have loved and who love you greet and receive your soul into the universal rays of light. By surrendering the mind to the natural embrace of the universal love, the process becomes a joyous experience of returning to the formless state of being.

The issue of thinking one is a famous master/teacher.

There are many who have seen themselves in their meditations or in a mind-created visualization as a famous master/teacher and then believe they are that being. What has actually happened in most cases is that the meditation presented a vision of the "archetype image" of a frequency of consciousness, and not a personality. Be careful how you interpret your meditations and visions so as not to personally step aside from who <u>you</u> really are. There are also other tests along the way. One of them is not to believe and trust everything you see and hear in meditation. Developing discernment is a profound skill to achieve, and you will be told after the fact in meditation that you were right not to take the vision or message literally.

These are just a few of the difficult issues facing people today. *I have shown that resolution can always be obtained through knowledge and love. The truth sets us all free.*

SANCTIMONIOUS WISDOMS

As a safeguard, there are several "sanctimonious" wisdoms or misconceptions that need to be revealed so they do not trick you and perpetuate any level of blindness or misdirection. Often the message or concept is filled with beautiful language, yet a subtle and effective limitation to the mind is taken in. Relax and be open to the following thoughts and see how they have supported the silent oppression of keeping people from being free in the universal love consciousness. Learn to develop true "thinking" over just having "thoughts" going through your mind.

Acceleration of time.

This collective concept that human time accelerates is not true. What happens is that a renewed participation of the people occurs. As they become active, the increased action makes it seem that a lot is being achieved and compacted into a short period of time. This contrasts with the slowness of the past and therefore is perceived as time acceleration. There can be cycles, like the seasons; just as when passing into spring it can make the winter cycle look like time slowed down, in reality people had simply been having less action and participation with others.

Vortices have powerful energy and make me transform.

This concept is used quite often and has no true value. The supposed vortex or power spot has equal energy to that of any other spot on the planet. The only difference is human-defined beauty, temperature, weather, human culture, etc. and of course, the lack of human psyche/mental energy around. The only true vortex in the universe is the divine energy of love. It is always all around and within you. It becomes known when you are ready to and/or make time to discover it. Many discover moments of the love energy when out in nature or in a particular human defined "spot," but *the energy "awareness" comes from within you* and not the external vortex location. You become aware of its presence within and around you. It does feel good to go where humans are not, as there is a reduced sensing of psychic energy pressure from others around. Not experiencing the mind energies of others allows one to expand and be reprieved from this oppressiveness. Yet, many have their greatest transformations in the comfort of their own homes and not at the mountain top. It is not necessary to travel to far places to make time to be still and discover the timeless truths and love you behold within. Of course travel is fun and you can travel. However, ideas of times and locations are *just ideas*. The universe is a random experience and vibrates in the ecstasy of love everywhere at all times. It is not any particular spot. It is not Hawai'i, Sedona, Mt. Shasta, Egyptian pyramids, Machu Pichu or Stonehenge. It is the earth's overall energy of love flowing forward in universal oneness that embraces you and assists you. You see and feel it when you allow yourself the time to sense it. Many native cultures, present and past, still embrace and process using the energy of the earth. Learn to be free wherever you are, with people or without people, in nature or not in nature, in a well known place or in a uncommon place!

Codependent behavior.

This term has been used very widely in the past few years. In actuality, this is a false description. Each individual does what she/he needs to do. When she/he (always by choice) participates with others, there is an equal exchange of energy and action that supports the individual's needs whether positve or negative. One is not dependent on the other. One is dependent on one's own past and re-enacts from the impurities of that past. The reenactment affects all areas of living, not just the particular other person who becomes included in so-called "codependent" behavior. Your behavior is not dependent on the other's behavior but solely rides on you as cause. What you project is only a reflection back to you, and you cannot hold another responsible for your life. Realistically, people act from unclear and disharmonious past distinctions until the pain hurts too much, and then a request for sincere inner change is made.

Channeling masters, saints, space beings, etc..

The seductiveness of maya is very strong and exists in all that is around in ideas and in matter. Many are seduced and spend hours listening to channelings and thinking about the channeled messages. Channeling will only bring the listener the booby prize of "understanding" and the channelor the identity of another being rather than creating their own identity and embodying their own divinity. You see, it is easier to channel another's message and it is easier to hear the message rather than to create the knowledge of your own direct enlightenment experience and bring forth your own true gifts and pure love. It is easier to have a relationship with a space being (alien) rather than purify and be who you really are. Instead, make the commitment and take responsibility to transcend the seductiveness of channeling, times of the past, and the great stories that are told and be true to yourself and stand tall as the great master that you can embody! When you do so, you will not "need" channeling or channeled messages, because you will have grown into knowledge from direct experience. You can achieve this by listening to the soft wise voice deep inside you that is your eternal soul speaking to you. In this state you will dance in the cosmic consciousness, reunited with your soul.

Earth changes.

The hysterical cry of dramatic earth changes is false prophecy. The bigger the illusion, the easier to sell the illusion. The planet has been evolving for billions of years. Prior to human occupation and human history, the planet had eruptions of many kinds. Recent small activities on the surface have been interpreted linearly to expound a horrendous pole shift at or around the year 2000. Beware of false prophecy and those who thrive upon them. Not true. All occurrences are naturally in balance for the planet. Whether it be earthquake, fire, hurricane, flood or volcanic eruptions, the planet is expressing its natural harmony and balance. Because they create difficulty for humans does not mean a great shift is going to occur and wipe out the dark and leave the light. How could that be, when the law of the universe is rhythmic balanced interchange? The universe doesn't care, it just loves! The final burning of the earth, drawn ever so slowly back into the sun as it goes nova, will take billions of years to happen. The earth will not exist for humans. Carefully evaluate appeals to spurious or questionable authorities and hearsay. Trust your inner light, and your heart will tell you what is nonsense and what is true.

Healing the planet.

Many people and many "aliens" believe they can shift the earth and heal it or affect it in other ways. These are false ideas that give these people a false sense that they can do such. Through purification we begin to bond with the planet and therefore become aware of environmental pollution. We take steps to recycle, to not pollute, and to demand responsible action by polluters. We can only give the earth love and receive her love. She is such a magnificent energy embodiment, and she has profound powers beyond our understanding. Our efforts for raising the vibrations of the earth are best achieved by giving and receiving love and not believing that we can "raise her vibration" through our ideas of spheres, shields, injections, veil movements or light grids. All of these self-aggrandizing behaviors are more for ego gratification than gaia salvation.

Beyond earth.

Be not carried away to open stargates three galaxies away when the learning for this incarnation is to be here and to accept being a spiritual human. It may be easier to escape into fantasy than to face your unhappiness. It may be easier to communicate with alien entities than your own family. The light, however, lies in the ability to express love and truth each moment in the here and now to yourself, family and friends. Descend and ground yourself and join the dance on earth. Make earth into the utopia of your dreams. The other galaxies do not need your interference. Most have less developed hearts and suppressed souls anyway and can learn from us. Advances in technology do not mean that advanced consciousness goes along with the products and toys. Other universe cultures are guided by the divine love consciousness for their growth as well. The divine love benefits all life forms and can give the message of the sacred wisdom directly.

Sealing of the aura.

There is no such thing as sealing auras. If this was so, people would immediately transition, as the aura needs to breathe and constantly receive energy. To protect yourself, connect your consciousness with the universal love energy. This is the greatest gift for safety and security. Become one with the holy light and be blessed and graced by the power of its love.

Third eye is the all seeing eye.

One of the biggest reasons people have not received enlightenment is that they are taught to use only the third eye for meditation. There are many more energy vortices/chakras of the physical and metaphysical body. The third eye is only the viewing screen. The projector and film to this screen are located at the fourth eye at the back of the head. When this center is developed, you become adept at accurately interpreting and sending messages to the third eye and seeing the visualizations. The fourth eye interprets energy and actually will give all knowledge and love empowerment to you before the thoughts, words and sights. This, along with the heart center, is where great change takes place.

Kundalini exercises and initiations are necessary steps to enlightenment.

Contrary to what gets marketed to justify many teachers' positions on the planet, these exercises and initiations can actually inhibit enlightenment. They create a relationship *with the activity* rather than a deep clear and sincere expression from the soul to be bestowed with the holy light inflow. Many become lost in various practices when their time could be better spent relaxing to receive the bestowal of oneness. The simple sincere beingness to receive the universe's love is all that is needed.

You cannot experience enlightenment until you are completely pure.

This idea of repeated lifetimes in quest of enlightenment is accepted by many, as they have the misconception that they have to be completely pure to receive enlightenment and that it is a long search. Not true. The divine loves you always. When you are ready for the love, it will be given to you. You will experience the holy light. The challenge is to be in the light and the state of enlightenment at all times. This state of being does take purity, yet can be achieved gradually!

I can only experience regression with a practitioner.

It is not necessary to be guided into regression beyond your first time or first few times for practice. Let yourself relax and ask the universal love to guide you to the perfect place in your soul memory to review for learning. You can easily do this with a friend or group, but it is not necessary to pay over and over again for these services. Practice builds confidence in your own skill development.

Baptism and holy communion can only be administered by an ordained priest, minister, priestess, spiritual teacher or other certified "holy person".

True baptism and holy communion occur by your own soul union with the universe's love. This direct experience is a personal communion with the sacred light in the "privacy of your soul". The certified ones establish purpose for themselves with these rituals.

Humanity thinks that ownership and possession are the natural order of things.

The only thing you truly own is your spirit with its gown/robe of light. We only rent and share our resources on the planet. So, let us be good caretakers and live more simply together. As one enlightened master said, "Why do you westerners save enough money for 1,000 lifetimes?"

Cotton, wool and silk are the only materials to wear for spiritual growth.

Perhaps organic cotton is the most harmonious fiber when concerned about wearing clothing. Just be aware that any fabric, regardless of color, is a layering to the body. No type of fabric will inhibit your receiving of the holy light. The light in the beginning can be consciously seen flowing in through the crown of the head. (Whether you have a hat on or not!)

I should be celibate along my spiritual path.

When you express physical union and tantra by relating with love, it is pure and fulfilling. You need not be celibate, but embrace relationship as it teaches you how to grow with another. If you want a concentrated period of time for spiritual inward concentration, you may choose celibacy, but remember how grounding, balancing, and joyous sharing the union with a loved one is. It is not only to learn to love thyself, it is to learn to love your beloved, also.

An ascended master comes from a lineage of masters.

A person becomes enlightened through surrendering to the light and releasing separate self-identity and ego. The reunion occurs directly, and one does pass through the pure and sacred light to the center. The ascension occurs by will and has nothing to do with whom one has known or been generationally involved with. There are many masters who are unknown and who live simple lives oblivious to the meaning of lineage. A true master experiences no negative emotions, has no ego and has fully integrated the soul. A master does not rely on "Hollywood depicted feats" to mesmerize the follower. A true master bestows love and truth only. Beware of teachers who claim they have been taught from an "ascended master" to "sell" themselves as an expert to the masses. Perhaps the learning is to master being a "descended" spirit living on earth and give love and wisdom.

Why is God treating us like this or letting this happen?

The universe is in a constant state of ecstasy, unconditional love and rhythmic balanced interchange. Natural occurrences such as weather and other "natural disasters" are not acts of God. They are the outcome of interactions of opposite paired energy forces within God's will for balance. War, sickness, poverty, hunger, etc. are created and supported by man, not God. These are driven by choices and distinctions that man and the collective culture have created. God only emits pure divine love.

The word "God."

When the patriarchal institutions "rewrote" history and their books, the Goddess was deleted. In this modern day, the use of the word God portrays a male holy source and does not represent the female. A new term to better define what God is, as God is unconditional universal love, would be **DIVINE LOVE**, which stands without gender connotations.

My master is a master, as he/she demonstrates metaphysical feats.

Special effects and theatrical mesmerizing hypnotize many. These demonstrations create a class system that separates people into followers of a teacher. Creating objects out of the air in the palm of the hand or making paint or other material appear on a canvas miles away does not bring one into enlightenment. It only appeals to the senses and creates admiration rather than spiritual acumen. *True masters do not demonstrate, they give love and grace.* They share wisdom and bestow the light. They will also do as all do - - when hungry, eat, and when tired, rest.

The devil and hell.

Fear and separation are created by these religious ideas to suppress the masses. In reality there is the unenlightened self that contains impure thoughts. It is within each person until transformation purifies the being. When in the negative and unenlightened consciousness, it can at times be "hell" within. The negative emotions are experiences of hell, as hell is not the state of heaven or love. The dark or shadow side is the non-angelic part of the self which one learns to master.

I am a walk-in.

Some people believe that they have "walked-in" and taken over a living human body as the original soul departed at transition (death). This is a false belief. The original personality has either become a multiple personality or is mentally operating from another area of itself and therefore believes itself to be a "new" person. This happens when a person gives their power away so completely to another part of themselves that they are operating in an ungrounded and fractional framework. Through building self-esteem and setting proper boundaries, the person can regain themselves within their body and recover a complete healthy mind. They will then not need the fantasy idea of being a walk-in as an identity.

The new world order.

Throughout time universal law has pervaded. It is humanity that has to convert to this law. The new world order is not government and banking oligarchy. The new world order is not new age fantasy that prosperity and everything will be just handed over to spiritual people and the darkside will disappear. Both of these are not grounded in the eternal solid foundation of universal law. When individuals and groups function centered in universal law, then and only then, will the true world order be experienced as fair, caring and pure. With each thought and choice, you are faced with building your own world order. Let it be the choice of universal law and the loving balance it presents.

There is a masterplan.

When you live in pure love and bliss, you will know there is no plan. The activities of divine action will occur as they occur in the present. You can sense the forming and create in thought and all will be successful. You provide the way. You are not controlled by a masterplan. You are radiantly riding the inner wave of sacred energy wherever it flows in the caress of love and your independent will of random interactiveness. There exists divine order in the universal law of rhythmic balanced interchange, but no masterplan. There exists love. Love is what there is, that is all.

These are just a few of the most common misconceptions that are promoted and supported in society. It is for you to use your discernment to learn that only love and truth are real. The love and truth are learned from direct participation with the light. This in fact creates the knowing of the love and truth. I invite you to break through to the truth and bypass the many ideas presented on such a wide scale to those who are on the path. I invite you to establish your own knowledge and the appreciation of your own knowledge. The power is knowing thyself!

QUESTIONS ABOUT SPIRITUAL AND ESOTERIC MATTERS

Insights are obtained when one feels pulled or directed to the truth. The inner direction brings one into the universal knowledge naturally. Perhaps the following common questions asked about spirituality and life have been inquiries of your own. They are asked over and over again by people. The answers are simple ones and perhaps will give you a sense of freedom inside.

Which is it? One life or reincarnation?

Both, with explanation. We do have one life throughout eternity and our spirit moves in and out of body forms and in and out of formless energy states in the continuing perfection of our existence in the rhythmic balanced interchange. In meditation and in the near death experience, one can see the loving light that we move into in our formless state. You have one life with multiple incarnations.

Which is it? Was mankind formed by evolution or the creation theory?

Again my answer is both, with explanation. The light has created all species, and all species have bodies that have evolved through time. The soul occupies each organic and inorganic matter with the spirit of the light. It is not one or the other, but both.

In what dimensions do enlightened beings operate? How many dimensions in the universe are there?

We all, evolved or not, operate in only one dimension - *reality*. Comprehending it or not is another conversation.

What really is ascension and where does one go when fully ascended?

The word "ascension" is being used by many in place of enlightenment. It is being interpreted and used to mean reaching higher states of consciousness and body and soul enlightenment. When one is fully ascended, one does not "go" anywhere - one just integrates divine love consciousness and experiences oneness with all. It is not higher, it is a purer state of consciousness.

Ascension is also being used as an idea that one can leave the body and transition at will and leave the planet. Groups have been led to believe that this will occur on certain designated dates. Do not fall for such fantasies. The underlying choice is truly deciding whether one wants to accept being here on the planet or not. This is a misuse of the word ascension.

What is the true definition of collective consciousness?

Collective consciousness is not as it seems or as it is assumed to be understood. Collective consciousness is the same as universal oneness/wholeness. The universe vibrates and exists in the constant state of ecstasy of love. When one is "consciously aware" of universal oneness, not by the understanding of the idea, but by direct experience and knowing that is achieved from the state of full enlightenment, one knows that there is no separation of consciousness. It is all energy and thoughts of love. One of the greatest misconceptions is that collective consciousness means "all human minds - including the unevolved". Yes, we are all connected and connected in love. No, we are not demonstrating "true collective consciousness" with non-loving, disharmonious, negative emotion and ego-driven thoughts. These thoughts are the thoughts of unevolved humans who are actually in "separation" and not in the "collective consciousness" of love. Yes, there are groups of people with like thought and like projects and goals, but most are not based in integrity and love. The ones that are, are noble and in true collective consciousness.

Where or what is the center of the universe?

When one is in alignment, the center of the universe is within you. When you become fully enlightened in the universal love consciousness, you realize that the center of the universe is not only within, it is everywhere. It is in the holographic atom of every speck of energy and matter. You feel the oneness with all things, seen or not. It is *bliss* to know this!

How do you tell the difference between God the Father/Mother, the Lord God of your being and Oversoul?

You will know them as one great energy that is so sacred and holy that you know you have integrated divine love consciousness. Contact is felt as love, sometimes profoundly so, and its true wisdom guides you, when you are willing, into alignment with the divine. It is holy light energy, not in a gender form, emiting strong wave sensations of love.

What do the aura and chakras of a fully enlightened or illumined being look like?

The chakras expand into one large unit of aura energy made of the universe's light energy. This massive field continues to grow in size and illumination as the being continues to grow into more potent levels of the sacred energy. In the final state of divine love consciousness, you know you are one with all.

Why are we here?

Why are we anywhere? *There is no difference as to the form, time or place in which one finds oneself.* Do you see? This is not about anything. We exist and we can live in love or choose to live in suffering. There is no meaning, as the universe is always in ecstasy. So, why not be in the ecstasy of divine love in every moment?

Why are there so many religions, cults and sects?

People want to believe. When people take personal responsibility for their spirituality, they discover religion is not necessary. Faith and belief are not direct knowing, and yet they are promoted by institutions to support their programs. There are also many cultures with varied languages in the world establishing and supporting different belief systems. Much of the information is manipulated to control the masses and to serve the religious hierarchy. The universe knows who is in truth and who is not. You can fool people, but you cannot fool the light! The effective groupings and individuals are the ones based truly on divine love, universal light. They give the individual the support and tools for direct experience. There are a few that operate from purity.

Treat others with kindness and express the honor you hold within. It is not for one to build great structures. It is to re-structure yourself to emanate love. Learn not to worship, adore and displace oneself to another class, but grow in your awareness of your spirit and live from the centerpoint of your soul self. The demonstration of spiritualiy is what is valued.

What are the virtues of enlightenment?

It was the age when music, song and dance were celebrated and used to portray advanced stages of consciousness. The parade of people wearing colorful patterned costumes blessed our sight depicting the various temptations of the world. The other solid colored costumes represented some of the many virtues of enlightenment. Although the annual gathering always started at dusk, candles and the full moon shed light and shadow in such a way as to enhance the tale of the path to purity.

Even the texture of the fabric was part of the message. Smooth silks woven with patience and love were revered. The hand embroidered images carried through the messages. Each costume was worn by its maker with honor and dignity. There was full participation by everyone, as all understood the secrets of life.

So, asks the inquirer of today, "what are the

virtues of enlightenment?"

My reply is that they used to be known as part of the culture, as in the one just described above. They were part of the custom, language and way of life. For modern people, the interwoven make-up is no longer available and a fractional lifestyle of distorted patterning is the foundation instead. Before one can truly absorb the definition of the virtues and behold and use their combined energy, it is important to situate one's mind in a new space utilizing meditation. In the new space, you will be more able to release what you have learned and allow your real identity to surface and realign with the timeless virtues of enlightenment. This new space supports you in living in the ancient, yet always fresh wonders of the universe.

To obtain the stature of one who lives utilizing the special forces of the universe takes tremendous focus and commitment in the beginning as one starts to form the initial realignment within. Each virtue that has to be relearned or just allowed to radiate freely, once again surfaces to be consciously reclaimed and used. So, the virtues can easily be identified by a teacher. However, it is a wise student who can see which are developed and which are not. Simply giving a list of virtues does not really serve anyone. My position is to direct and teach you the rediscovery process which is worth more than merely reciting lists as answers. Do you understand what I am saying?

Let me answer your question further with another question: Would it be more effective if you could identify within yourself which virtues were strong and which were not? Would you then proceed to strengthen the weaker ones? The list of virtues of enlightenment would only be a piece of paper with letters in certain sequences and of no actual value. The value is in your own analysis of where you are in your own stage of development and in what direction you could grow further. My answer to your question is, *Which virtues do you need to enhance and how can you do it?*

Which should I do - pray or meditate?

Methods may not be the same even though the *same descriptive word is used.* In general, prayer is an outgoing wish, hope or desire. Effective meditation is both an outgoing and incoming communication. At deeper levels the exchange of pure divine love energy occurs. Both work well when the individual sincerely acts from the heart and communes with the divine love energy of the universe. I would choose *sincerity* over the method, as it signifies the communion is from the heart.

The Buddhists and the Hindus speak of the place of emptiness. What is this?

For many religions and groups, the place of emptiness is the goal and is called the "enlightened place". In the divine love this is the "starting" place for enlightenment. When you meditate and go behind the words, visions and all thought at the place of the fourth eye, you come to the sacred energy that is still and holds all knowledge and peace. By learning to use this divine energy which is the place of emptiness, you can direct the energy to expose past misconceptions that the mind still holds and from which it creates negative emotions and separation. The truly enlightened master is in the sacred energy at all times, in each moment. The advanced state of nirvana, samadhi, cosmic consciousness, trinity or divinity is living each thought, action and no thought in the divine energy that is never empty . . . . it is love.

How and why do we incarnate?

After our planning and selecting the womb in which to be embodied, in a precious moment of pure love, the soul softly enters the womb on a ray of divine light. We incarnate to remember our love and to love and be loved. Incarnating is part of the balance of rhythmic balanced interchange of universal law - the constant cycle of formless to form, form to formless, formless to form.

Is man more advanced than animal, insect, plant, mineral or water life?

This is another old human invented conversation. Because one can process more information does not mean one is more advanced. Let us define advanced. Is it a being that lives in balance? Is it a being that can take care of all its needs? Is it a being that has a larger brain, yet makes unbalanced and unloving choices? Look again around you. A tree is a pure energy field of light just as a crystal is. Animals adopt observed behavior, and most animals pass on the standard behavior of their species. Are dolphins more advanced because of their abilities and because they play with us? Are whales, owls and deer more advanced because they live in their natural rhythm? Is water holier than air? *It is not the body that determines "advanced", but rather the action when in or out of balance. So, if any being lives within the law of balance for its species, it is advanced.* If it throws other life forms out of their natural balance long enough, the other forms will perish.

Is it their purpose to destroy the others, and is this in balance for their species? Humans, perhaps as an instigating species, are the lesser. What happened to the "caretakers"?

Why does risk into the unknown or taking a risk feel so uncomfortable?

Sometimes it seems that everything begins to stagnate and one is directed to the only direction to go - take the risk! What is risk and why do we feel fear and resistance around risk? Why do we sense impending loss or damage with risk? Is it really taking a chance or is it something else?

Risk does not exist where there is love, and where there is love there is knowledge. Being careful and cautious is wise, but not when it begins to block evolution. Whether the risk is a small one or a large one, it holds the potential of change into the unknown. The unknown results may or may not be to your liking, and you therefore want to know the outcome before taking the risk. But only through risk can one make change and evolve. To uncover your underlying ideas and thoughts is risky, as it may entail changing your perception of yourself. Your foundation for your identity may shift, yet you find yourself wanting to be secure in what is already known. The already known past has already been lived and gives you your present results. If you want your results - your world - to change, then new knowledge is necessary to bring you into more awareness - therefore, go forward into: risk.

When the discomfort becomes painful enough, one desires change. Your journey and processing along this journey brings you to a choice of risk. Whenever one is faced with risk and it is the direction to follow, one knows that great achievements can be made taking this step. The new step out into the world to a more supportive way to enhance your life will not be a risk for long. For in your consciousness you will understand the aspects and parts that your soul wishes to bring together into a completion form. The completion form will help you realize you are taking care of your needs and fulfilling yourself.

Reaching your goals takes participation and new expression. Relax your mind and allow your soul to expand and feel the love in your heart. Allow your energy to expand and feel centered within your heart. Go to your quiet place where your inner voice and vision can speak to you. With this divine embrace, listen within. Feel your sensations around risk and the unknown - about embarking on new paths and choices - and instead of resisting the change, ask your mind to be guided by the soul and the purity of the soul's essence. Let go of any fear or unrealistic feelings and begin to rely upon the soul's knowledge within to discover reality and clear the way. Trust this reality, and it will guide you safely and directly to more of yourself and provide you with an enormous return. It will set you free by giving you permission to grow into your true soul self. Begin to trust yourself.

CHAPTER THREE

WALKING THE TRUTH

WILL AND THE WORLD

It is appropriate to explain a few things about living in the world and how it operates for our benefit. We are all led to believe that we have a purpose to achieve. It is our divine heritage to pursue that which enhances our stay and promotes our evolution. It is also our right to be here and our responsibility to participate with genius. We are not here to ponder and wander. We are here to attain and direct with our genius. It is the same to do here as it is to do in the rays of light. There is no difference, only in how we sense our world. This world of form does appeal to our senses in different ways and operates on the same principles and rhythmic balanced interchange as the rest of the universe.

It is not for us to amass large quantities of information but to challenge ourselves and learn knowledge. It is not for us to amass large quantities of money, enough for a thousand lifetimes and not share it. It is not to be so worldly but to be holy. *Knowledge is in fact the soul teachings of the divine love energy that empowers the entire universe. The search for knowledge is not an outer project or achievement but an inner finding.* It is not in the outer world we will find the truth but in the inner life. The world can only give us feedback as a reflection of our inner knowings.

As you unveil and participate at deeper levels of the pure consciousness, you learn that you are in the world to teach the knowledge to others. This enables the blessing to continue and eventually we will all live "in the world" as divine beings. How we discover our part and self-knowing is up to our own free will and desire to know. The world does give us many stimulants and distractions. To sift through them takes a strong will and desire to learn that it is not them, but us, that we need to sift through. After letting go of the outer world distractions, one can then sit down and "focus" on the study of the self. This is a major achievement, as the world does mesmerize and use up many years of our lives. It is genius that awakens within to inspire us to play and dance in the journey to self-discovery. *Listening to your will is a powerful stand to take, as you give up being led by the world and decide to lead your world.* Once you conquer and claim your wholeness and come into enlightened living, you can teach and share with the many your insights and revelations to assist them.

There are no delusions or illusions - only our needs and desires of the day. If we are unclear, we need to be unclear. If we are lost, we have needed to be lost. If we need love, we will find love - real love. Whatever we need and desire we shall have. It's just that so many do not desire and do not ask to have their needs met - they have given up. They have stopped living and participating and begun to wither. They lose their smiles and the sparkle that was once in their eyes. Until, one day . . . when they hear their inner voice again and turn themselves on through the desire of love, self-expression and fulfillment. It is totally up to the individual to shift. It is our greatest gift to the light to grow in the light and return to our wholeness. The world is our home as much as the invisible ether is. Increase your will by becoming inspired by your inner light - let your love speak and your heart dance. Be in your joy and plan what steps you will take to lead your self-destiny into the divinity of universal love!

TRUST AND NEGATIVE EMOTIONS

"Responsibility in confident expectation of oneself or another" is a brief definition of trust. As one grows in love awareness, one's trust and confidence grow. Or is it, as one's trust grows, one grows in the love awareness? Walking across hot coals of fire is an exercise that tests and helps one to trust in oneself to accomplish a task. If you can do that, can you create other breakthroughs? You need not pay large sums of money to build self-trust in the universal love energy. It lies within you and can be revealed and unveiled with each new knowing of oneself in divine remembrance and through self-achievements in the world.

Trust is not something that is earned. It exists inside and is given. How much you give shows how much you have at a conscious level. How much you receive is a reflection of what you give. To trust is to give your love. To love is to trust. Yet, how does one create more love and trust in themselves and in the holy light? Why do people inch their way to transformation instead of empowering themselves to dive into it? Is it fear that prevails instead, slowing the evolution? Why? For what end? What? *Give power to fear - and not to LOVE?* Why stay in fear and not trust yourself to take the risks to evolve?

Using the tools of the divine energy to rediscover and to know the underlying causes of fear takes a strong desire and will. As each cause is reviewed, it is easily erased from the holding of the limited mind - and one becomes free, free to trust in the area that was previously unavailable to trust in. As we learn that we have chosen each experience in our past, we learn what our purpose or reason for the interaction was. We have done what we have needed to have done throughout eternity. We have blamed others for the symptoms, but true realization unveils our reasons for participation in the exchanges. We are in total control of how we have been treated. We can either allow the situations and negative emotions to run us, or we can choose to run our lives.

When one takes the responsibility to run one's own life, change begins. The ability and desire to trust in oneself starts to return and be strengthened. The divine remembrance (soul memory regressions) meditations of our past start to reveal patterns and choices that recycle themselves until cleared with love. The birthing of inauthentic ideas and distinctions are understood and erased forever. The mastery starts to take hold. A new clear and radiant being surfaces from underneath these deep hidden thoughts and shines in trust and love to grow further. Great jewels of wisdom are received.

It continues to build and build. The inner courage grows to such an extent that you can clear your entire past and no longer be in separation and ego. You can clear and surrender and release yourself completely into the arms of love consciousness. You therefore erase and master the limited mind and ego. Whether you are used to hearing this state being called enlightenment, nirvana, samadhi, cosmic consciousness, or trinity, know that you can become a being of purity. Your growing trust in yourself will enable you to come into your true and pure natural state of divinity. It is for you to decide how you want the outcome of your daily living to be.

Growing up in the world gives many experiences of distrust, hurt, sadness, limitation, etc. Because of the buildup of so many rejections and moments of fear for various reasons, people get used to not being accepted, trusted or loved. The pattern repeats itself over and over in personal experience, on TV, on the radio, in the newspapers and magazines, in books, on videos, in commercials, everywhere. No wonder people end up being lost in the maze of negative treatment and depictions. To be able to take a stand for self-development is a major accomplishment! To stand and say, "I do not want to live like this anymore", is a profound shift. Just this stand is a huge step to self-knowing.

Where does one begin, once the stand for self-love takes place? There are many choices. Some are extremely valuable, and others are not very good. *You will create what you need at each step of learning. However, please remember that change occurs inside of you when you want it to happen. Regardless of modality or system or exercise, you will create the change when you are ready to.* You can choose to trust yourself and grow in little increments or in big leaps. You can choose to give yourself opportunities and time to grow quickly or slowly. The achievement is based in your self-trust. If you think you are going to die going into the unknown, think again. This is an amazing block to carry. Where will you go when you discover fear, anger or inner pain? You will *feel* and *expel* the *cause* of the fear, anger and pain. And then what will happen? *You will feel a sense of release, clearing, freedom and knowledge in that space.* So, tell me, where will you die, or where is the risk in the unknown? *The unknown is actually the opportunity to gain knowledge which leads you to a present state of truth and love.*

You can challenge yourself with trust-building action. For example, I would actually sit down at night and tell myself that in the next hour I am going to tackle this problem I know I have. It would be like a homework assignment - as common as that. I would do this over and over again to clear my past negative emotions. This is what I call responsible commitment and action. After a while, you start to run out of things to work on. So then what do you do? You play and dance in the paradise of life!

Do you want another example? Why don't you try visualizing yourself jumping off the planet Earth (This is a bigger challenge than a cliff!). . . ok, stop reading and take a moment and face your fear and let go to do this exercise. . . Do not read further until you have tried this, or some other idea for trusting yourself is demonstrated. All right, what happened? As you jump off the face of the Earth and free-fall through space, the sacred light flows out as a beautiful ray of love and sweeps you up into the center of itself! The light is always with us and receives us in and out of bodily form over and over again. What is there to be afraid of? Do you think you will not be there to catch yourself? You are always with yourself as an eternal soul, so how could that happen?

As you review your past, you may want to make a list of what you do have trust in now that you didn't before. You will realize that each shift really was previously being held in an idea that did not support you. Learn to rephrase your thoughts to only reflect statements that will *empower* you. Change the ones that do not into empowering statements. They will show you where to look for clearing and growth.

Most people deny self-discovery, as they do not want to confront or feel negative emotions. The denial blocks progress and limits one's development. What are the negative emotions? Here are the most common ones: anger, apathy, boredom, depression, fear, frustration, grief, guilt, hatred, impatience, insecurity, intolerance, jealousy, loneliness, lust, nervousness, pain, pride, rage, sadness and negative stress. All of these harbor past experiences that inhibit the receiving and giving of our trust and love. Each is a great signal and teacher for us to connect with its origin to purify. Each is based in inauthentic interpretations of circumstances, and the interpretations create mental distinctions that we can carry with us through the ages. It is in your desire to trust yourself that you can face these, understand the balance of the experiences and transcend them one by one. And, there's no better way to do so than using the universe's love. When you receive the unconditional divine love energy, you receive nurturing and comfort to your soul, to your heart. This warmth gives you the power to face the emotion and to process it. Follow your heart and break through the mental and emotional barriers you have created in your head and free your heart! Be in your joy and learn to grow in your trust and love of yourself and the divine energy. All the keys to your happiness and success are held within you. Listen to them now in your universal love meditations and learn! The serenity and security that come are priceless!

TELLING THE TRUTH

Know thyself in the universal divine love consciousness! Tell your truth and uncover the suppressed areas that supported the negative emotions in the mind. It is in your review of your past through divine remembrance that you can see what has caused the negative emotions and what distinctions the mind held. As you complete your remembrances, you will purify and discover that you feel more freedom and love with each clearing. Soon, all clearing has taken place through telling the truth and you no longer live in the mind or the negative emotions. *You live in the union of the ageless truth in full divinity with your soul in its natural complete state.* Telling the truth allows you to live from your heart and to express love freely. You become sincere to yourself!

To tell the truth and to get to know the truth takes considerable courage. Do not settle for partial awareness and live in subjectivity of the future times in negative emotions. Trace your past and reveal the causes of certain impure thoughts and erase the weakness of the mind and its control. When you live in the ageless truth, you do not control. You have surrendered to the universal love instead. Your powers are truth, love, freedom, compassion, joy, humor, relatedness, peace, harmony, softness, innocence, wisdom, strength, and leadership. These powers enhance your being and are naturally restored and integrated as you unveil your soul. Live in your soul, which is centered in your heart. You will have a completely opened heart and resonate with the vibrations of ecstasy as the universe does.

When you tell your truth and live in the truth, you do not care what others think of you. You actually live in the way, the truth and the life that totally supports your needs. Your self-esteem is healthy and strong. You are self-directed by your ageless knowledge and wisdom. You can see the light in others and their distance from fullness in the universal divine love consciousness. You are able to support them to take steps to shorten the distance as you can see where they can enter to be enveloped in the love. You no longer need or have the ups and downs. You strive for the constant smoothness of enlightened living, and it comes to you as the integration takes place.

I encourage you to tell your truth. I support you to rediscover who and what you really are. Go beyond your current identification and journey into the deeper realms of consciousness to know yourself completely. To help you to see the power of the truth, I will share two divine remembrance experiences of my own:

"One life in particular was very challenging. I was the daughter of a holy guru and lived in the temple up in the mountains. I was being trained to carry on the sacred work when my father transitioned (passed over). I was shocked, as I had not yet been fully trained. I didn't know all that I was supposed to do and felt abandoned. I had to lead the masses as best I could, and deep inside I felt uncomfortable, as I was incomplete. It was a difficult time for me, but the people didn't know.

They were happy to be at the temple and to be guided. Later, I brought the divine love and its light into the temple and became a fully enlightened being of sacred energy. I was thrilled and proud to have been 'self taught'. It was then that my father came to me in spirit and told me that this was my lesson: 'To be responsible enough to learn and to become one with the light by following your inner soul directly with the divine energy!' Later in life I passed the temple on to my daughter. I taught her to keep her soul open and unveiled and to function from holiness at all times."

Ever since this divine remembrance I have been confident and directed to be public with my services. I feel comfortable to participate on a wide scale with my speaking, writing, etc. This is why I say, review and tell your truth. See who you have been. My truth is and has always been to be a self-taught being of enlightenment consciousness. I have the remembrance of doing it before. The other divine remembrance experience is:

"I saw myself as a holy man and head teacher of

a school for lamas at a monastery. Each student became brighter and brighter in the light as I helped them into enlightenment. As I grew older, I passed on my role to a student who was just so naturally bright, and brighter than the others. I trained him for a while and then knew my life purpose was achieved. I left in the comfort of my sleep knowing I had continued the teachings of divinity for the lama school in this ancient life."

I am now living my truth and expressing the ageless wisdoms that come from universal consciousness and my divine remembrances. I am empowered by seeing who and what I have been before. The truth does set you free beyond your imagination. Do not be afraid to take the steps that will create your dream life experience. Tell your truth. Walk your truth. Use the universal energy to guide you to your past, embrace them and emerge with wholeness fully into the present with presence.

MARKERS

When a chart is made of the "great markers" or the big steps you have taken for transformation, it will show how much or how little you have accomplished over a period of time. In the understanding that we do what we need to do, some of our needs take decades to achieve while we sacrifice other important ones to be attended to at a later date. Typically, mid-life crisis depicts a later date that comes to face some people in their 40s and 50s.

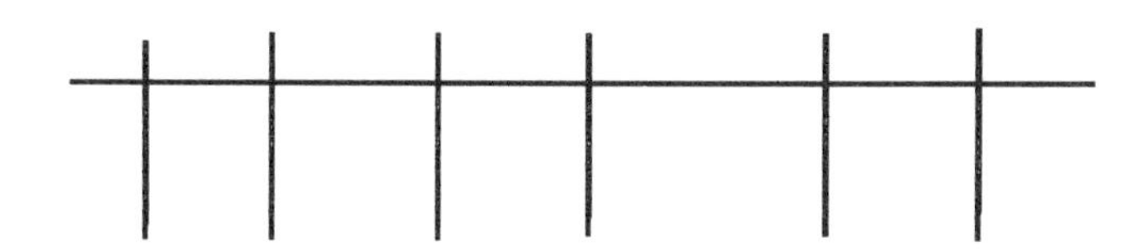

Kindly get a blank sheet of paper and draw a straight horizontal line all the way across. This will be a linear chart. Remember the very first spiritual or metaphysical experience you had or any first real conversations about spirituality. Make note of those to the extreme left of the line. Work your way forward on the line (to the right), using small vertical lines crossing the horizontal line as date markers. Under each date, put a brief title or summary of the experience. Work along the line to include up to the present: breakthroughs in learning, overcoming fears, receiving profound guidance, being with the universal loving light in your meditation for the first time, seeing your spirit guides, major dream messages, shifts during bodywork, special relationships, self-expression, etc.

Now, review the markers and enter anything else that you may have forgotten. Look at the time that has passed since your first experience. See the gaps for long periods between experiences. Do you see where you could have accelerated your growth by focusing on your growth instead of other things? What were the needs then that kept you from your growth? What worked to give you concentrated periods to do more growth? Digest your overall analysis of your marker chart and institute a plan to give yourself the time and opportunity to support your growth for the rest of this year.

Let's create another marker for your chart. Ask yourself, "What am I suppressing now? What is underneath my limitation? What can I do to give myself permission to have ____________________ in my life, etc." Follow this issue in your divine remembrance regression and pursue the underlying cause(s). Learn from the review and pull out your life purpose and life learnings for that time. See how it relates to you today and feel the transformation that has just taken place. Add this growth to your marker chart.

I have found that each marker is most often a review of a previous incarnation. Past limited thoughts do hinder today until one is completely purified. Other markers are clearings of negative emotions and negative stress that are held from past experiences as well. As you purify by mastering the emotions of the mind, you will see that the markers give you a clear record of your transformational history.

The overall picture will most likely give you inspiration to do more and accomplish more now. This increased incentive will continue to build as each experience brings you more love and power. Your self-knowledge will begin to drive you to complete and be free and end the journey at the beginning in universal consciousness. It is up to you to focus and commit to achieving your wholeness by making the time and effort to do so. It is well worth the commitment. To live in love in each moment is an ecstatic state of consciousness. It is like your endorphins are going off all the time. The universe naturally vibrates in this ecstasy of love. Build your desire to clear your past by focusing on knowing yourself. Use the sacred love to guide you in each review. This is a very quick way to develop and succeed in meeting your goals.

BE FREE TO LOVE AND TO TRUST

Often, many are reminded that their daily lives are not or do not appear to be the way they would really love to be living. There is also a feeling that there is no other choice, so the sameness remains. Not so for the ones who live in the wholeness of love. For it is the unconditional divine love energy of the universe, its light and sweet presence that embraces, nurtures and guides your unfoldment to be free. To choose and to trust, to learn to live as love, and to grow in the receiving and regiving of love, is a major achievement in these times. Having the will and desire to take responsibility for one's destiny into purity is "genius". To be determined and focused to create a new life based on love, joy and peace is an immeasurable and eternal gift to oneself.

Even though many do pray, commune and meditate, often it leads to a cycle of words and visions and not to the additional deeper levels of soulfulness. To invoke and infuse the integration of love requires full reintegration of living from the innocence and integrity of your soul. The greatest shifts and changes are the result of consciously loving oneself enough to receive the soft waves of unconditional love from the universe into your heart. New expanses of freedom and improved self confidence occurs. These enhanced powers will continue to stimulate further consciousness awareness, focus, and the grace to trust and love yourself and the universal love even more.

It is through and by this magnificent love that you can begin to emerge and authentically radiate your natural inner light, and your profound gifts and tools to express in this life. You will discover that living in your body on the planet is just as beautiful. rewarding and joyful as it was when you were in the formless spirit state. There is no difference between being here or in the light, as there is only divine energy and its light of love, within and without. So, all in all, *you can transcend with love and trust to be complete and free!*

CHAPTER FOUR

LIVING THE LIFE

YOUR WORD

How many words per day do you speak? How often do you keep your word as spoken throughout the day? Is it loose, lazy, kept sort of open, uncommitted, unclear, etc.? Do you change what you have said? Are you heard? Do you listen to others' words? Are your words just sounds without promises, direction, commitment, follow through, power, wisdom, affection, compliments, praise, etc.?

What is your word? How can words empower you and the world? Is there love and peace in the sound of your voice? Even though some of you may have forgotten, in each moment when you give your words you can give the vibration of holiness in your breath and sound. You can reach into the souls of those around you with your speaking when it emits love.

There are many models of speaking without the love principle. It is up to you to discern to live without this sound and surround yourself and model yourself in love principle communication. For as you speak with love, true knowledge comes forth. It feeds everyone. You ride along in the same direction as the flow of the universe. Life is easy by your word. Retrain yourself to speak in this new way throughout the day and enjoy the dance of sacred living. It will show in your eyes, your smile, your overall body language. *Newly prepare yourself to be treated with language that contains the winning principles of the universe co-created within.*

INTUITION

Intuition has often been defined as a hunch or a premonition that mostly women feel. No further thought is really given to this activity. It is looked upon as something that happens randomly and rarely. It may be grasped fully or it may be a fleeting, confusing "notion" that one tries to tie to the future or associate directly with the now, as you are thinking a thought. It is something that even the experts are in a quandary over. What is it? Can it be developed and taught? Why do some people have it and others not?

Intution is defined by the sensitive one's as inner psychic ability. They believe it can be developed and advanced. Then you need to define psychic. What is it? Can it be developed and taught? Why do some people have it and others not?

The secret is not that intuition and psychic ability are the same, the secret is that intuition is expressed when one hears and sees the universal energy with the mind set aside and the soul in interactive communication directly with the pure universal energy. This is when truth is uncovered. Prophecy is reading through the soul, with all circumstances as they are unfolding, giving a probability of a future occurrence. The accuracy is execellent by professional seasoned readers.

What intuition is best used for is to discern people and situations to guide you to make the best choices with confirmation from the pure universal love energy. The universe loves to assist with knowledge and wisdom exchanges if you only reach out and ask. Your inner requests are heard when you speak sincerely from your soul. It is your soul that will guide you to yourself and grant your greatest achievements in life.

I request and listen for a complete reading on all those that I come into close relationship with, whether for social or business purposes. It gives me accurate background on the people and I can discern my involvements in advance. When I receive that a person is "reliable", I am confirmed to commence a business relationship. When I receive that a person is "full of problems", I do not commence a relationship, as they have to be clearer to be in my immediate presence. The intuitive process allows you to hear the soft honest inner voice of your soul. Trust it and listen to it in quantity.

People use different formats to communicate the messages. Some use psychometry, cards, pendulums, numerology, astrology, names and dates, and others use nothing, only their energy. To each their liking and to each their years of experience developing their mastery. I see your energy and translate it into words and visions. I, also, receive on your behalf messages and visions from the universe to bestow. It has always been a clear and easy access since my very first meditation in 1980. 1980 was my time to reawaken to my spiritual life and mastery. My gifts to the world are my insights and revelations that empower and grant self-awareness and freedom. I have no limitations and can read anyone or any idea anywhere in the universe past, present or future. I know with sound and vibration movement in your voice when you are not telling the truth and when you are. I have been tested and there are no tests that can trick me, as I am integrated fully with the universe and my soul is fully unveiled and expansive. Whatever you do, call it intuition, psychic or ignore it entirely, it doesn't matter to the universe. Your life choices are your life choices. This book is a summary of various aspects of the human process and is only a model for what can be.

Intuition is a very stimulating human skill and faculty. Grant yourself confirmation for your life choices with the experienced intuitives and psychics. You will feel support and comfort in the guidance alignment. Their gifts expressed on your behalf is their fulfillment and purpose.

THE SACRED CELL

The cells of our bodies vibrate naturally in sacred energy. In this natural state, we are healthy and well. The divine order feeds our bodies with pure unconditional love. When we restrict this energy flow and hold what is not of knowledge or what is not true information inside, our cells become repressed and their relationship with the sacred energy becomes limited. The loss of remembrance of the universal consciousness and how to live in the holy principles unbalances the cells and their environment. When great losses of love energy participation are incurred, people manifest illness and diseases. Each illness and disease exists from certain misidentifications, misrepresentations and untrue distinctions in the mind. The way to purify these thoughts and to be in wellness is to listen, think and speak from the soul - from the heart - and the love. Love rebalances the cells and their environment, and wellness returns.

Even though it may take years, decades, or multiple incarnations for the unbalance to become noticed in the physical body, it can be rebalanced in a very short time. Our ability to understand and know the causes of our symptoms can be seen in our divine remembrance. Our soul carries all of our past thoughts and experiences. We can access this profound knowledge and memories to change our limiting patterns and to empower our unlimiting ones. To succeed one only need to look inside, recall and feel. Track the energy of the vibration, relax into it, and ask your soul to guide your memory to the perfect place for learning. When you feel you are ready, open up your inner sight and hearing and review the memories that developed the symptom(s). Ask what your life purpose and learnings were; see if you achieved them. You can sequence forward or backward to get full frames of additional viewings for more knowledge and information. When the review is over, ask to sense your thoughts and feelings when you transitioned or moved into your next form. You can additionally ask to review with your spirit guides, in a spiritual board meeting, and hear what you had discussed and planned. The soul will help you process quickly and give you the timeless truth. It is the greatest teacher and friend one has, as it is one with universal love!

There are keys and tips as to why one has a certain ailment. They relate directly to the energy vortices of the body and to the receiving female left side or sending male right side of the body. Let these placement areas help lead you to the knowledge held within the ailment. The extent of the holding is in direct relationship to the intensity of the thought or idea. This suppression limits the flow of love energy and we start to wither. The body is a great reflection of our thoughts. Listen, watch and learn from its many messages and be guided. You can create remarkable shifts immediately by loving yourself and allowing the love to fill each cell and flow as it should.

The sacred cell extends to all organic and inorganic things. They are all a part of the wholeness, and at the same time each is the center of the universe. If we feel, think and act with sacred energy, respect, honor and kindness, we will be treated with the same. It is up to us to be the example and to initiate the giving of these powers. It is our demonstration that gives our fulfillment. Be in the sacred love energy and share this love with all organic and inorganic things. Your computer and your car appreciate loving thoughts in their service as well.

The sacred cells of the cosmos all participate together in the ether and in their expressions of form. They combine in a rhythm and dance in their gravity, holding each in the ether with their superior beingness. The universe is perfect. It is human interpretation and meanings that support human concepts of "imperfections". There are no imperfections in the universe. The sacred cells all vibrate and operate in the rhythmic balanced interchange. Rhythmic balanced interchange was defined by Walter and Lao Russell, of the University for Universal Law, Science and Living Philosophy by saying, "God gives you the right of free will to think any thought or perform any action, but He holds the right to balance your unbalance by an equal reaction . . ."

Your will is a divine gift. It is your free will that makes choices that inhibit or heal your cells. The state of your wellness is the reaction or effect of your will or cause. The reaction can be positive or negative to your wellness, emotionally or physically. If we can keep charging ourselves with the universe's divine love, we will be illumined and reflect the perfection of the love. Our balance can be wholeness and wellness in our entire being. We can radiate the love and refuel ourselves to regive and to receive in the regiving of love. Let us learn to create powerful equal reactions like - light to light - and - joy to joy! Your cells will recall their sacred memory and be nurtured and healed in the balance of wellness and love.

There are many developed special ones that can aid your journey. They have mastered the universal love powers and provide healing energy to support you. Their advanced abilities will help you to short cut your growth and to build your own direction and authority. Ask for their guidance and assistance. You will find a friend in their wonderful and noble service.

FOOD AMONGST THE FLOWERS

Food is a major part of the day and of our being in the world. There are very simple secrets for a nutritious and harmonious diet. By responsible choice it can be economical, simple, quick, easy and health supporting. It can be gentle and peaceful to other species. Imagine eating all you want every day and never gaining weight and maintaining a slim figure with strength. Imagine easily being able to digest your meals, putting an end to indigestion and feeling sluggish. Imagine not being a part of the process that continues the slaughter of animals, fowl, fish, and their eggs and milk. Imagine contributing to feeding everyone in the world by no longer feeding the grains and corn to animals and then eating the animal for food. Why eat food that has already gone through other species bodies?

There are six authors that have excellent books for sacred diet and health. They provide full details of the benefits derived from a vegan or vegetarian diet. It will change you life when you read the facts and pull away from the commercial propaganda that the public is fed each day. The propaganda perpetuates the slaughter and perpetuates disease for humans.

Anne Wigmore's book, The Hippocrates Diet and Health Program is endorsed by Dennis Weaver. It is the "raw living foods" diet that I live by. Daily, I eat several small meals and drink plenty of fresh squeezed juices. I am satisfied with very little and usually average only 1-3 food types at each meal. I buy one-fourth the amount of food I used to buy when eating cooked vegan meals. I am feeding myself live fresh organic nutrients in the best way and my body gets satisfied with less. I do not eat any form of sugar, syrup or honey. Only dates, raisins or figs for sweetness. My pancreas loves me! When you feed your body fresh nutrients it will not want excess. The average diet gives signals to the brain that it is still starving for nutrition even after you push down large amounts of "cooked and processed foods".

The second author is John Robbins. His book is May All Be Fed. He gives you the shocking facts about dairy products and animal products, how they are obtained, processed and how they negatively effect the human body. He also covers how the current food distribution system keeps the hungry around the world unfed and under nourished.

The third author is William Dufty and his book is Sugar Blues, published in 1975. It is an eye opener about the sugar industry and how it is so bad for your body.

The fourth book is Fats that Heal Fats that Kill by Udo Erasmus. He has tremendous information about the processing of oils, what happens when they are heated, how the body cannot tolerate them and which ones the body needs for health. You may not use your wok again.

The fifth author is Dr. Norman W. Walker. I really like his book Fresh Vegetable and Fruit Juices, as it gives combinations of drinks to strengthen and heal the body naturally.

These authors have other books that are very important to educate yourself about food and your body. Learn why our bodies love fresh fruits, vegetables and nuts. When you feel good you have the energy to go further inside to hear your inner voice speak and you are a brighter light expressing yourself in the world. When we have guests staying in our home, they change their lives in this new direction as they experience how delicious healthy eating can be.

My favorite dessert recipe book is Sweet Temptations by Francis Kendall. Try the raw living foods carrot cake, apple pie and nut torte. They are awesome. It will show you how wise nature is. You can show nature how wise you are by making your contribution to the environment and other species with your alignment with the knowledge the above books contain. Treat yourself to the truths they have found and treat yourself with love by honoring your body with nature's best -- the food amongst the flowers.

LIVING AMONGST STRANGERS

It is a very funny human phenomenon and accepted cultural attitude to be "living amongst strangers." Not just with other human beings, it extends deep into the individual personal psyche, as well. Is it not strange to not communicate or know your neighbors at home, work, and play? Why are we not greeted and welcomed by our neighbors when moving into a new building or neighborhood? Do you not know people in the church, institute, clubs, and associations you belong to if they begin to exceed a certain size? Can you even remember the names of everyone? Would you like to know them? Would you like them to know you? Do you want more close friends? Are you shy? Do you prefer privacy? The Delphic Oracle, Pythia said, "Know Thyself". Do you know yourself? Who are you, really? Have you become a stranger unto yourself?

It is easier to live in the not knowing for those

who live in larger populations. However, this behavior even extends to small towns and very rural areas. People take the former mindset with them. And yet, when you have ventured out to make that extra contact you do feel a sense of satisfaction and recognition. Even if it is just a smile, you have acknowledged each other's presence.

People also attempt to protect themselves from harm by not meeting other people. Do not limit yourself. Use your discernment to protect yourself and your family and you will be safe. Additionally, there are times when your neighbor does not seem to have any common interests and they do not interest you to further the sharing. However, do say hello and introduce yourself. There could come a time of need or common interest and your relationship will have already had the foundation of your first greeting created.

As you know, superficial relationships are not satisfying. What are the underlying factors that support this behavior? Is there not enough time to relate and care? Are you only thinking of yourself or your family?

Can you bridge the gap with taking the lead and opening the conversation up? Are you willing to develop friendship from nothing? The rewards are great and very worthwhile. Pursue the riches of friendship and stop living amongst strangers.

Even though life is quite personal, you will be appreciative when acknowledged by those whom you had not known. Even if you let it be just an acquaintance, it does have the exchange of neighborly consideration and care. Extend your kindness to those around you and feel comforted that you have created communication that takes the other and yourself into a beginning. Your identity is partly made of those around you who greet you. Greet them back and reenter into a new pattern of making time for human basic acknowledgment. You will be respected for your breakthrough of the barrier amongst strangers.

FRIENDSHIP AND FAMILY

How my heart sings and my soul dances when I think of the word "friendship". When we are free to be who we are, we attract wonderful people into our lives to share and enjoy our lives with. It is a great pleasure to hear your friends' voices, laughter, breath. To listen to them and to share your speaking with them gives fulfillment of self-expression and supportive acceptance. It confirms who we are and who they are as well. Listening is not better than speaking, and speaking is not better than listening. They are both equal expressions and the content, spoken or not, and will communicate the message in energy. The co-creation for friendship, love and learning together is a "tribal" privilege that we all initiate and nurture together. Gathering feeds our souls and supplies many of our needs through networking and exchanging.

To develop a gathering of friends extends our

light fibers to bond and mirror with others of like vibration. This is how we can strengthen collective consciousness in the physical world. We have the opportunity to reach out and bond with extended family. The focus then permeates as a collective energy to generate the vision of the grouping. Our souls are joyous together as we grow together. This active and enlivening participation is a remembrance of ourselves when in the rays of light. The light is made of divine beings bonded in energy as well. It is natural to be drawn to friendship amongst spiritual beings. When you surround yourself with spiritual friends, you not only enhance yourselves but the divine energies as well. We are all united in the kindred spirit of the heart - the universe's divine love.

The depth of friendship love makes me speechless as I recall how full my life is. The feelings are so profound that the energy radiates past the words. I can only say to you to not let these opportunities pass you by, by enveloping your days in worldly activities that buffer you from the depths of friendship love. The power of being loved and loving is a blessed gift as we actualize on the planet. To have your heart open is such a stimulating sensation to be in. Expand this within your being and allow your soul's center at the heart to unfold and blossom further. The endearing moments we can share with our friends are our cherished memories of the future.

With our friends we can be vulnerable and share our thoughts and secrets and aspirations. They can help us to succeed and prosper. *The sharing can be so deep that there is no separation.* You can experience deep loving relationships of light energy here. This way of living becomes a sacred way of life.

To select with discernment whom one plays with or does business with can insure continuous harmonious living and long-term relationships. Discernment is a powerful skill that develops with a commitment to do so. Watching and listening for behavioral patterns in those we interact with eventually builds an understanding of their character and degree of authentic living. Through divine love one can be very compassionate to others' states of being, yet a line or boundary can be set to indicate whom to include in one's inner circle of friendship. This boundary of discernment can be used regarding people with whom association is needed to carry on with daily business activities as well. In fact, this is such a powerful skill that my divine complement (husband) and I share our discoveries and therefore eliminate enmeshment with those of unclear energy.

Our friendships prosper by modeling the pure and sacred standards of the benevolent universe. As light attracts light, our friends attract friends with the same standards of excellence in friendship expression. We hold each other with our bond of love. They know we are there for them and they for us. As Joan Grant states in her book, Eyes of Horus*: " In friendship both must profit equally, for when one profits nothing neither can the other, so it is assured that you will learn from me for you have so much to teach me."

*Ariel Press, Canal Winchester, Ohio 1988

Learn to move from living in separation and isolation to including oneself in community friendship. We are here for such a short time. Make time to co-create friendship. Generate opportunities to meet new people and involve yourself in a larger circle of friends. The networking that evolves from the new associations gives you new avenues for joyous participation, learning and prosperity.

We have all had many incarnations where we were included in society as a whole. We had deep affiliations and dynamic relationships based on the collective community's needs and our personal needs. We have experienced the profound sharing of goods and services exchanged with love. This is in our divine remembrance. If the desire is present, one can attract this same way of living by evolving and attracting others who wish to express themselves in the same manner. Harmonious living comes from within. It is a powerful choice to make this commitment to one's existence this time through. Change happens within your heart. To support a sacred lifestyle requires coming from the heart.

Some of the new participating friends in your life you have known before and some are truly new associations. Each is a part of the whole with so much to contribute. As you grow in the love consciousness, you increase the love that you have to regive to your friends and family. You experience a spontaneous joy to give your love and to share this divine energy. You are fulfilled in the giving and blessed in the constant grace of the divine love inflowing to your soul center at the heart. Living in love and joy brings you to dance in the light, and there is no journey. There is only the presence of love; there is only the present to be in; there is only the brilliant oneness of the universal knowledge and its many gifts. Behold the grand splendor of your being, held in the loving arms of the divine love's light.

To make a friend one must be prepared to be a friend in return. It is here that the weakness lies amongst the human species. Rather than align with the positive attributes and morals, many are drawn to the defective aspects and inferior character qualities. Some of these negative traits are brought into this life, some are learned from family members, some are established with the affiliation of impure persons or initiated within the self. Many people establish a relationship that strengthens the weaknesses, and through time they become more pronounced and hurtful. Many project their personal agendas onto others and restrict "what could be" by virtue of their limited awareness. There are takers who are non-givers. There are always signs along the way during the newness of relationship. Watch for these signs and for the words that the new people use and for their actions. What are their daily practices? Do their actions match their words? What have their past actions been? Do they have good family communication and relationships?

So, as you develop new friends, use these discernment skills to see that you are creating powerful alliances that support your growth into the light and that support your desires and ideas. It is these relationships that will stand through the tests of time and contribute to your successful unfoldment to true self. It is these friendships that we name the "100%ers", for each gives no less than 100% to the other. This giving remains constant and does not waiver.

Your great friendships will respect and honor you. Your great friendships will trust you and be there for you in times of need. Whether the need is emotional or of sharing energy, your friends will be by your side, anytime of day or night. Learn to rely upon your friends and unite with your hearts to grow your friendship together. We are not here to be alone and to self-provision our needs. It is so much easier to combine as a group and enhance our experience here. Enjoy your contribution with the others of like caring and concern. Feel safe and secure and free to be vulnerable and soft in their love. Open further and surrender to the wonderful times and pleasures of true friendship.

In addition to friendship, we have our relationships with family members and children. Our families are here to help us learn to communicate, love and build friendship as a practice field. For, if one can love the family, one can love the friends. Family gives us a tremendous opportunity to express our love and give beautiful modeling to the other members. Passing on the powerful sacred principles to family benefits us all. This leadership will help to shift our culture into a positive and harmonious one. We are given, by choice, our families that we are born into. We have had friendship and family relations with many that we surround ourselves with today. We know each other from very deep remembrances. There are many standards, purposes and dynamics that synthesize in the selection of the best birthing channel and household through which to come into form. The co-created matrix for your best opportunities of growth is well planned. Your role, life purpose and life learnings are all bound within this matrix for your interest in reaching your goals.

Some move through life with more than one set of parents - natural, step and/or adopting. Some have to clear their inner issues and unlearn behavioral patterns of multiple sets of parents. Whatever the relationships are, and regardless if connected by blood or not, people never forget their emergence from the divine love light deep inside. The love is our eternal and universal parent, friend, clone, guide and playmate. It is such a grand experience to be enveloped in the light and to manifest into our physical bodies. *We are all children of the divine energy.* Enjoy this opportunity to be in the physical universe and grow in the divine consciousness. Live in bliss each moment. Share your light with your friends and family and know that each giving of your love, regives to us all! Live your life to its fullest!

PROSPERITY

Prosperity, wealth, and success seem to be very popular topics; not surprising in a capitalistic society. Some people seem to be good at self-provision, and others have a difficult time. It is genius to establish prosperity fulfilling one's life purpose and not just performing a "job". Some of us have never lived in a civilization where self-provision was based on a common exchange system like money, rather than sharing and bartering. To learn how the system of common exchange works does take practice.

My divine complement and I know that we have all the riches of the heart, and our lives are enriched by our sharing of our knowledge in our services. Because we are modeling what we teach, this authentic embodiment of the divinity does bring us prosperous living. We are free and not limited by erroneous distinctions of the past. We are unlimited in our manifesting abilities and therefore open to receiving prosperity. As we regive the love and the knowledge, we are regiven successful living. Pure prosperity is obtained by providing a service or product that has value which allows for a sustained giving and regiving, in balance.

If self-provision has been difficult, use the universal love energy to take you back into your soul history and review what causes are still holding limiting blocks to your success today. Releasing the impure thoughts will bring you into your power, your gifts and your prosperity. You will gain insights to the laws of the universe. The following is another example:

"A past life experience that I reviewed to evolve in my prosperity expression occurred in 1400 B.C. I was a spiritual seer advising a woman of great notoriety, position and power. We had a long relationship of successful vision and planning for the region. I was also very public and well known. Unbeknownst to me, her two sisters were jealous of our friendship, and they viciously murdered me one evening. At the time of the murder I drew an erroneous distinction in my mind. During my regression I heard my inner voice say 'If I become public again with my power, then I may be murdered again.' In all future lifetimes and until recently I lived less visible, quiet lifestyles doing my teachings and visionary guidance. Once I remembered this incorrect distinction (the meaning) my mind had carried from the past, it was gone. I automatically replaced it with truth and love. I was then able to separate my interpretation and meaning from what really happened. I had been expressing love, truth and wisdom publicly and I eventually transitioned by murder. That was that and it didn't mean anything about this lifetime."

Ever since the remembrance I have been confident and directed to be very public with my spiritual work this lifetime and have prospered naturally. There are many examples of blocked prosperity due to past erroneous distinctions that are carried forward. People have misused money and in their next life they do not want to have anything to do with money perchance they misuse it again. Others are afraid of success because it will enslave others. If you are not in prosperity there is/are thought(s) that are blocking your flow of energy with the universe's.

All the success workshops in the world will not bring you to unlimited wealth unless you can indeed reach inside to your personal history and clear the false distinctions that fuel the mind and its holding of negative emotions and repressed living. It is for you to be responsible to bring to the surface any impurities and to progress yourself into enlightenment. Hearing of your past from another will usually not clear it. Your own personal regression will, as you will see it for yourself and own it. There are usually only one to three personal deep misconceptions that keep people from pure consciousness living and prosperity. There can be, however, many lifetimes recycling the limited lifestyle that is based on the misconception(s). Regress and overcome.

I ask that as we enjoy our wondrous and magnificent self-created lives together, we honor certain principles by including and maintaining them in all transactions with ourselves and others. These are a few of the divine principles for prosperity:

1. Request and model loving equal kindness to yourself and all parties known or unknown.
2. Create a positive gain for yourself and the entire grouping/community.
3. Insure an equal exchange of value to all participants.
4. Commit that each part of the whole is being responsible for others that may come up short.
5. Provide an ability to repeat and continue the giving and regiving in universal balanced supply.
6. Dare to portray and educate particulars based in true facts.

Remember, where there is win/lose there is not love, there is survival. The new world order can learn from this. *You will always be blessed in holy transactions that include loving collective continuance.* I embrace you with universal divine love and wish you a comfortable, sacred, and successful journey into prosperity. Grow in your worthiness, self-esteem, and ability to receive and develop your gift to give and be compensated. It is easy and simple to evolve with the universe guiding you. It just takes priority time to devote one's attention to the self. It just takes focusing to clear one's past to become present. Release your past with the divine love and release yourself into the divine love. Surrender to the truth and to the love. Surrender and release and be one! Be free at last to be successful! *Those who come to include universal law will live in balance and peace.*

DONATIONS AND TITHING

There are natural givers and there are people that can learn to be givers. Natural givers are noble in that they understand what it is to share and what the sharing will bring. There isn't an attachment to money or possessions like the non-givers have. Their inner knowing contains a feeling of security that we are all in the flow of the dance with the universe. The inner knowing contains the knowledge that the giving and sharing is a major contribution to the whole, to the betterment of the oneness for all.

In The Message of the Divine Iliad * by Walter Russell, he says the following:

> The seller of goods is also a buyer. If the seller gives less to his customers than the value of what he charges, he deprives his customer of the ability to regive that which the seller needs to again become a seller. By sacrificing the good-will which is the foundation of continuance in any business, the love principle has been

*Walter Russell Foundation, Waynesboro, Virginia, 1948. p. 77

subtracted from the transaction in the measure of inequality of interchange.

Neither man nor nation can continue an interchange of relation upon a harmonious basis of multiplying power when the universal love principle is violated. The law of balance is absolute. He who breaks that law will be equally broken by it.

If each of the two conditions which form the basis for every transaction between pairs of opposites in nature can be kept in balance with the other, the resultant effect is *good.* When they are out of balance with each other, the resultant effect is *bad.*

Good and bad (sin, evil) measure the degree in which pairs of oppositely conditioned effects of motion are either in balance with each other or out of it. In all our human relations we ourselves make our own good and bad (evils and sins), by our desires and decisions to act either in, or out, of balance with Universal Law.

By example, what Walter Russell is saying that if people provide services on a donation basis either as an individual or a non-profit organization, the society can create balance and give in the regiving of power and love to these people to carry on for the whole. On the other hand, by choosing to regive nothing, an imbalance is created and the service may no longer be available to serve anyone. I say that each being can meditate and come from the truth of their heart in the giving process.

Donate not from the mind or the pocketbook but from the truth in your soul's center at the heart for each instance. Measure not the services from the mind and from comparisons to others' fee structures, but measure from the purity of the loving soul and the desire to create a balance for the value received. You will know by using the inner energy to quantify and be in the living of perfect balance in all interchanges.

Know that many are invaluable and beyond measure. Some are not yet consciously understood to even measure at the moment. Give and know that in your giving you are regiving to yourself and the entire universe. Teach others how to become givers and re-direct the selfish direction into an outer direction of community. You have many deeds to be done. Give of your deeds, tithing and donation. You will remember your gifts when you transition as a measure of oneness. You do not give to the person or the organization - you are giving to all consciousness, and in your giving you are renewed.

COMPASSION

In universal divine love consciousness, there exists great compassion. The compassionate being can listen and support those in need and who are still in the journey. Along with instant appraisal, the teacher is able to guide the person toward their truth and to the purification required to transcend and evolve into an enlightened being.

Although compassion is a developed skill and by-product of enlightenment, it is a great gift to grace those that come in contact with the wise one. Just being in the presence of great compassion can open wonderful gateways of knowledge by providing arenas of expansion to grow into. You can excel and expand in the essence of compassion.

Approval and acknowledgement are additional by-products of compassion. When in the presence of compassion, you know that you will be loved and nurtured. You will not be turned away for who you are, for what you have been or where you are along your journey. An open-hearted master is such; an open heart for you to be embraced and accepted by. Compassion will extend the love energy to you and guide you to embark more deeply and become more focused on your path. You can receive insight and confirmation from compassionate teachers and friends. Let yourself receive the compassion and grow in you own compassion. Do not forsake others. Grow in your compassion for others and for all species and matter. Demonstrate your growth by increasing your compassion, by giving yourself permission to break through the inner barriers that have held you back. Learn to be compassionate to yourself! Compassion is not something that is only given to you; compassion is something that you regive to all around you.

CHAPTER FIVE

OPEN LETTERS

Know that you are loved. Feel the precious qualities of the universe. *ORACLE*

Dear One,

It is your destiny to be unencumbered by a culture based on and driven by armed power and capitalistic idealism. The true creative process does not include these pervasive controls, whose ideals do not nurture the natural balance of the universe. True creative expression births itself in purity and is given and received as a gift from the whole to the whole.

It is for you to unlearn the past and shed its limitations. Begin anew, renewed in the great embrace of sacred love and peace. Enliven yourself by unfolding your inner light so that it shines upon us all.

You really have only one gift to give - love. Then, all action can be based in its loving expression. Cherish this gift, as it is the only one there is.

You have more to do, so start to connect with your true identity and walk away from your unreal self that betrays all universal laws. This is the forever moment of the present, as it has always been, to call upon your awakening once again. Stand tall in your heart, let your eyes shine and your smile be seen. For in the silence, all begins unencumbered, by design from within.

With blessings of love,

ORACLE

Dear One,

Domination is a strong trait amongst the human species. It exists in more ways than people are willing to review and change. It is so pervasive that it is easier to look the other way. If one ignores this state of affairs, one is subjected to its domination. Children and adults dominate, institutions, governments, cults, ideologies, rules, laws, theories, developments, cultures etc. dominate. It is everywhere. What does it take to understand and see past this structure to something else, something to replace it with, and how to replace it?

In the sea of love, domination does not exist. There is no air for it to survive. For in love, you are treated with love and you are coming from love in all of your participation. There exists a wellspring of support for your love. The wise one gives you space to be. You are welcomed to let go of the common game and allow your pure self to be expressed. You develop your awareness and use your advanced intelligence to out smart the dominating structure to a level that satisfies you. In this place of satisfaction you are free of the mass agreed upon game. You choose to disengage from all of the propaganda and subliminal messages that pound the public all day long.

Yet, some still ask if you beat the system are you not then dominating it? Be awakened by the fruits of the sea of love. If you need to ask this question, it means that you haven't embodied love to its fullest yet. When you do, you will see the overall universal picture and know that you have stepped out of the spell of human domination behavior. *Live through non-attachment and you will be free. Learn to grow above it and live in a kind and caring environment.*

Benevolence grants peace,

ORACLE

Dear One,

Know thyself as divinity.

Be courageous each day.

You are the pure essence of love.

Be love and be loved,

ORACLE

Dear One,

As we travel through time, know that the holy essence of our souls are joined together. You are not alone, as we are with you in spirit and in love. Be bold and discover your gifts that are to be shared as gifts. You too will see that inner breakthroughs advance all of humanity. Your growth blesses your soul and everyone else. I honor your careful choosing and committed expression to each choice as you evolve.

Joyously being,

ORACLE

Dear One,

Have no fear.

Bestow the word.

The word is love.

Love,

ORACLE

Dear One,

You have read my words of the timeless divine love of the universe. Unite with your inner truth and expound your ideas and expressions with your love. Do not suppress and limit yourself in any way. Go forth and be who you really are. Receive the unconditional embrace of the universe's divine love energy and radiate your profound purity to all.

I have given you my knowledge and I rest in the knowing. We are all one!

Blessings for your soul's journey,

ORACLE

AN INTERVIEW WITH THE ORACLE

What is an Oracle?

I have been described as one who speaks for the universe and is the touch of the universe. The quality of the universal knowledge and wisdom is pure, expresses true principles and works well with the individual's soul development. The service of an Oracle is devoted to assisting each person by revelation, insight, confirmation and empowerment to obtain divine living and fulfill-ment.

How did you develop your skills?

In my first meditation, in February 1980, I was visited in spirit by a great spiritual master who glowed of such deep love - shined through my heart with golden rays of light. It was the turning point to begin my life's work.

Only three months later, in May, I realized the intense mystical enlightenment experience (a.k.a. nirvana, samadhi, shibumi, holy trinity, ascension, cosmic consciousness, seeing God) many religions speak of, by sincerely asking to receive the universe's unconditional divine love. By January 1994, I evolved to an advanced state of consciousness by fully mastering the emotions and the ego. I am now one, in awe of each moment and with each thought - - free.

How do you work?

I have been graced with the gift to bestow the universal love energy and its light so that any person can see, feel, receive and integrate with it in a group gathering. I combine the bestowal with the deep inner knowing of their soul's truth and support them to acknowledge this empowering remembrance and move into the positive teachings and strengths of the divine love wisdom. This brings inner peace, strength and enhances the overall wellness of the person. My great joy is seeing their increased awareness, fulfillment and heart felt happiness in the universal love.

There are no separations between the unconscious, the subconscious and the conscious mind. I work with the soul of each person to awaken and unite clarity, intelligence, balance and oneness. This allows the mind to surrender completely to the soul. The soul then can unveil fully with its truth and love. It is amazing to know what profound knowledge and sacred integrity the soul reveals from within. It helps each person to co-create with the universe the life they always dreamed they could have. Your intentions start to manifest with continuous infusions of the sacred energy. The journey ends and the search is over - you emit love and live in enlightened universal consciousness!

Do you hold seminars?

Yes. "The Oracle Teachings" seminars and "Evenings With The Oracle" are currently presented with love in California, Hawai'i, Arizona, New Zealand and Australia. We are happy to travel and share the knowledge. I feel very blessed to meet the sincere seekers of the light. It is a joy to illuminate the divine essence.

Kindly use this convenient reply form to contact us.

Yes, I am interested in further information on or would like to order the following:

______Attending or sponsoring **The Oracle Teachings** seminars or **Evenings With The Oracle**

______***The Oracle Speaks*** book,
US$12.95 plus US$4.00 shipping

______***The Oracle Speaks*** on two audio cassette tapes,
US$19.95 plus US$4.00 shipping

______The Oracle's 900# Personal Growth Phone Line

______Please send 8" X10" b/w photograph of The Oracle,
US$10.00 each, or US$15.00 with autograph,
includes shipping.

______Please add my name to your confidential mailing list

* Add 4.165% sales tax for shipping to Hawai'i addresses or 12.5% GST to New Zealand addresses.

Name:____

Address:____

____

City:____

State:______________________________Zip Code:__________

Country:____

Phone:(_______)_____________________________________

ORACLE PRODUCTIONS LTD

P.O. Box 6146
Wellesley St.
Auckland 1036
New Zealand
Ph 011-649-358-4222
Fax 011-649-358-2197

P.O.Box 3300-393
Princeville, Kaua'i, HI
96722-3300
U.S.A.
001-808-826-7373
001-808-826-6633